The Promise of Christmas

THREE KINGS AND A PRINCE: THE FIRST CHRISTMAS

The Promise of Christmas

Three Kings and a Prince: The First Christmas

Dana A. Lagmay

Library of Congress control number   2011905351

ISBN   Hardcover   979-8-9852700-0-6
                Softcover   979-8-9852700-2-0
                E-Book   979-8-9852700-4-4

This book is printed in the United States of America

To order additional copies of this book, contact:

Dana A Lagmay, The Promise of Christmas publishing
1 808 431-4118 or 1 808 639-1263
promiseofchristmas.com

Contents

DEDICATION

This story is dedicated to all of god's children young and old. I invite you to read and wonder if this tale from the heart can be true. So if you believe that angels are real, and fly from the heavens to live among us, then is it so far fetched to believe there truly is a St. Nicholas with a sleigh and reindeer flying though the heavens during Christmas?

To my children who have always been my inspiration; Joshua, Heather, Isaac, Dasha, and my grand children Brittany, Cherie, Jayben, Joshua Jr., Christian, Mateo, Apollo, Tatam, and Gabby, and all my grand children that may come after. I ask them to continue celebrating and believing in Christmas as I did, and as God intended, to give and forgive, to love unconditionally, to be a beacon of hope to those who are lost, and give shelter to the homeless, and to nourish their bodies and soul.

For God said, what you do onto them, you do onto me. And so it is intended that the proceeds of this book will start and help fund The Promise of Christmas Children Foundation, dedicated to help children of the world to know and enjoy The Promise of Christmas. I would like to thank my parents, Catalino and Ignacia, who raised me with a Christian foundation that inspired me to write this book.

I would like to acknowledge and thank Natalia, and her mother Vera, for their unselfish support in helping arrange research in Siberia, and for encouraging me to finally publish this book and all of the sequels to follow. And lastly, I give thanks to my dear wife Sharon, and my heavenly Father for his words and guidance while writing that will remind all of us, that the true "The Promise of Christmas," is Easter. For God so loved the world, that He gave us the gift of His son Jesus, to forgive all of our sins of the past, present, and future, to give us hope, happiness, lasting peace, and eternal life.

I would like to acknowledge and offer the staff at Universal Breakthrough a heartfelt thank you, and may god bless you for your efforts.

PROLOGUE

egend has it a star fell to earth and formed the large valley providing shelter for the town called Tobolsk which was built by fur trappers and traders. On impact, the massive explosion and upheaval of the earth's crust formed a vast chasm and, over time, created mountains and lakes in the desolate wilderness of the open Siberian tundra. It became a safe haven for all. They believed the fiery star pierced the earth's crust and continued to burn deep below the ground of the valley basin. Molten lava-like metal seeped out of the ground and cooled to shapes of rocks and branches. Mysteriously, and for reasons unknown to cave dwellers, their caves were always warm, providing comfort and safety in the bone-chilling wind and snow of the long Siberian winter.

The open tundra surrounding Tobolsk bristles with a wide variety of wildlife. The most sought after by trappers are foxes and minks for their fur, and the most feared is the great Siberian grizzly. Tobolsk prospers from producing fur of the highest quality. However, without any form of ruling authority, its prosperity attracts many who prefer to make their riches off the blood of others. The weak and poor, are prey for the strong and the wealthy.

Cave dwellers who first lived there centuries ago named the lake in the center of the valley basin Star Lake. Near the shimmering lake, in a large cavern carved into the side of the mountain, lives an oracle that is visited often by the villagers and their children who find warmth in his cave and sit around his campfire. The oracle entertains them with his ancient tales of a magical star, cave dwellers, and a prince who battles over the forces of evil. The cave had become a special place for the children to play. It is like an enchanted playground offering a place to explore near the safety of the village, and is always under the watchful eye of the cheerful oracle tending to his reindeer herd in the area. Living alone without a family, most people believe he is somewhat strange and sometimes crazy because of his clothes and the stories he tells the children. His clothing is a mixture of new and old woven cloths and fur, with a floppy fur-trimmed hat matching neither his clothes nor his shoes. He walks around with a long wooden staff using it as a cane, but not needing it to support him. While his clothing is not new, his appearance is neat and clean, and his shoulder-length silvery-gray hair shines like silk. His sparkling eyes, rosy cheeks, and cheerful smile instantly fill the empty hearts of the children who come to him often for comfort. He loves the children that come to play, and they love him in return because he is always cheerful and let them ride on his reindeer. While listening to tales of a prince, the oracle treats them with delightful snacks of roasted nuts and dried berries. During this season of long, dark, and cold nights, children find comfort in having their thoughts taken away to far and distant lands that can only be seen in their dreams, away from the bitter cold of the Siberian winter. As the oracle describes this faraway world, it is a land where the sun is as bright and warm as the star that fell to earth here in Tobolsk, and the sky as blue as the water of star Lake. Indeed all who listen to the story take off on a journey of adventure and wonder.

CHAPTER 1

Born Again

I am going to send an angel in front of you, to guard you on the way and to bring you to the place that I have prepared. Be attentive to him and listen to his voice

Exodus 23:20-21

A sandstone tower is silhouetted against a dark, gloomy sky, and reaches high above the fortified walls of the palace. The fortress protects the king and his family from any unwelcome intruders. Until now, no enemy could penetrate the high limestone wall protecting the palace. However, this enemy attacks silently and swiftly kills everyone in its path. Through a window in the tower, Princess Andrea gazes across the hazy, gray outline of the distant horizon through her teary, reddened eyes. She cries mournfully when she sees the smoke from the burning burial pits. The smoke holds fast to earth instead of rising, creeping along and blanketing the ground, as if goaded by bodiless spirits to hold fast and not leave until the last agonizing moment. The pungent aroma in the air is a mixture of smoke from the pits and rotting flesh ravished by the dreadful disease. She leans forward and gazes out her window, and below her, near the walls that protect the palace from attacking enemies, she can see the lifeless bodies of their servants, attendants, and soldiers from within the palace being stacked on flat wooden wagons to join the countless lifeless bodies of others from the city, making their final journey to the burning pits.

At the last full passing of the moon, she dreamed of having the most celebrated wedding to Prince Ezra on this very day, but now, it is destined to be only a dream, unfulfilled. Now that many before her have died from this dreaded and incurable disease, she senses that soon she, too, will be taken to the burning inferno. With her fingers—now void of any feeling and the blackened flesh at the tip of her fingers, announcing death's call—she writes her final letter to Prince Ezra, pleading to him not to despair and to seek out another princess who can share with him the happiness of raising a family and someday rule over his father's kingdom. When both were young, everyone felt they were perfect for each other, and their marriage would unite both kingdoms, making them powerful and their people more prosperous. Princess Andrea's beauty and charm were everything the prince desired. The prince adored her, and her beauty was unsurpassed by any queen or princess before her.

Ezra has a tall muscular body with a smooth and lightly tanned skin. His dark-brown hair fell to his shoulders in loose, glossy curls. His emerald-green eyes, high cheekbones, and stern jaw line disguises his tender and generous personality. He is a skilled warrior and, most notably, an expert swordsman and archer. He has also been schooled in other languages and astrology. The kingdom of Prince Ezra is feared because of their highly trained soldiers that keep marauding armies away.

On the shores of the great sea is the kingdom of the princess known for its commerce and trade. However, they were vulnerable to many travelers trading goods and animals. This had also exposed them to unknown types of diseases. When the plague overtook the kingdom of Princess Andrea, no one dared enter in the kingdom, and anyone leaving faced certain death from King Caspar's skilled archers of the neighboring kingdom. With all precaution, the king prevented his son Prince Ezra from visiting the princess, until finally, the dreaded message announcing the death of Princess Andrea arrives, and her last letter is read by Prince Ezra.

Ezra becomes so distraught. His life has no meaning, no purpose, and worse, no one to love and in return be loved. He remains in his room, not wanting to see or speak to anyone. He can only see and speak to his beautiful princess in the empty recesses of his heart while anguishing over his loss through long days and sleepless nights that turn into months.

While gazing out his window one night, he notices a star he has never seen before in the dark northern skies. He studies it for hours, observing the uncharacteristic way it sparkles and gleams. "Is it you, my princess?" he whispers. Then suddenly from the star, a brilliant flash bursts forth, and a bright fiery tail blazes across the jeweled black vastness of the skies above. His eyes follow the streaking ball of light heading directly towards him until it stops, and hangs suspended in midair outside his window. Bewildered and frightened, the prince rubs his eyes to be sure that he is not dreaming. The dazzling display of light astonishes him as he stands frozen with his eyes and mouth held wide open in awe of what he sees before him.

He is more surprised when he hears a gentle voice from the light calling out to him. "Prince Ezra, be still. Do not be afraid. Listen to your heart and follow your dream."

It has a calming effect on him, and he feels as though he is in a hypnotic trance, feeling spellbound. The voice tells him not to despair, for soon he will find peace, harmony, and happiness in the place where his dreams will take him.

That night, feeling hopeful that the pain and anguish will stop, Ezra sleeps. He dreams of a place strange and yet beautiful. The air is pure and the ground is covered in a white blanket of cloud dust. He is cold, and yet he feels the comfort and warmth of tranquility surround him. He finally awakens and realizes that unless he finds this place, he will never know comfort and joy again as he did before his Princess Andrea died. At long last, he leaves his room to seek his father's permission to go on his journey to find the place that will bring him peace and happiness.

Known to be a very wise man and hoping it will end Prince Ezra's pain and suffering, King Caspar knows it will be best to let his son go. The wise king also feels it is time to test his son's courage and knowledge. The king prepared his son from a very early age to someday leave the homeland and explore unknown regions beyond their kingdom. Armed only with the knowledge of languages, the stars, and skills of a warrior, Ezra, his horse Shamal, and a pack donkey with supplies, departs from his father's kingdom in his quest for peace. He journeys northward by following the star that spoke to him for many lunar seasons, until one day when he comes upon a land so strange, he thinks the edge of the world is nearby.

Tobolsk, Siberia Early Fall, 7 BC

Prince Ezra leans forward in his saddle, combing his fingers through the black, satin mane of his horse Shamal, and he speaks, "We must be close to the edge of the world," in Arabian, a language familiar to Shamal. The stallion anxiously paws the graveled ground and nods his head snorting, appearing to agree with his master. Puffs of warm air stream from Shamal's nostrils, rising upward to form clouds in the crisp frosty air. Shamal has been his trusted companion since he had received him as a gift from the king of Arabia. Being alone, without someone to talk to for most of the journey, it feels natural to speak to Shamal. In this unfamiliar land, Shamal seems uneasy and skittish, and Ezra's spoken words calm the mighty stallion.

Ezra steps down and stands amazed by the land surrounding him. The air feels cold as it was in his dream with clouds brushing the distant white mountaintops. It is strange and yet familiar. "Give praises to God! I'm finally here. This is the place of my dreams," he says aloud. Shamal bellows a deep throaty grunt while nodding his head upward above his arched neck.

Prince Ezra feels certain that this is the land the voice from the heavens spoke of. He remembers the bright star he had seen that night before leaving the safety of the kingdom and how it beckoned him to follow and appeared to get brighter each night as he got closer to this strange place. The towering, majestic mountains and rough, crusted landscape surrounding him feels eerie, and it sends a chill down his spine. He stands in awe at the base of the mountain, looking upward to the top, and then he notices a well-traveled path ahead of him, winding up its steep and treacherous side. A gust of wind sends waves of fallen leaves, yellow, red, and gold, rustling up the path. It is a sign that the season is changing. He remembers what Nicholas, his faithful servant and teacher, and Nubar the explorer, the trusted guide of his father, taught him of the nomads of the northern regions, who lived in lands such as this. He now wonders if the nomads live on the other side of the mountain that was standing before him.

Weeks earlier, while on a deep-rutted road, he met travelers he thought were nomads, with light-colored skin, fair hair, and eyes colored like the sky. They spoke the language of the northern nomads that his teacher Nicholas had taught him. They intrigued him with tales of a mysterious village hidden in a large valley in the middle of the tundra, but warned him to stay away from a large, furry beast called a bear. They said it feared nothing and had a ferocious temper with sharp powerful claws that could slice through men and horses while standing on its hind legs. He also heard of another animal even stranger, but very gentle, with leafless tree branches growing out the top of its head. They called it a reindeer.

Making his way up the steep, dangerous path is treacherous and difficult. The long journey of nearly four months has drained both himself and Shamal of all their reserved energy. Without nourishing food and rest for days, they are both hungry and weak. He looks for shelter from the cold wind and finds himself on a pathway high above a valley basin. The setting sun makes a wide arc, skirting the earth's rim, and slowly disappears below the horizon in hazy hues of purple, orange, and gold, casting dark shadows of the mountains in the valley below him. From the edge of a cliff, in a high narrow pass through the mountains, lantern-lit buildings from a town sparkle like beacons searching through the treetops below him. Storm clouds brewing overhead block his view of the bright star that guides him, and the twilight shadows turn dark and gloomy. "At last, a safe haven," he says in relief as he follows the road down the mountain pass. It is so cold; raindrops turn to white powder that clings to his eyebrows and lashes as he shields his eyes from the piercing cold wind. His father's most trusted guide, Nubar, had warned him of this. The white cloud dust blankets the ground, forcing him to tediously guide Shamal slowly and carefully or risk slipping and falling off the steep edge onto jagged rocks below. Death waits at every foothold.

Step after each treacherous step, they make their way down the narrow road. Shamal and the pack donkey carrying supplies slip and lose their footing often as they struggle to make their way against the strengthening wind storm. Deciding to walk and find better footing for his animals, he carefully places his weight on one stirrup to dismount. Then suddenly, shattering the darkness around him, lightning crackles directly over his head, followed by a deafening clasp of thunder that shakes the ground beneath his feet. Shamal bolts, and snorts fighting the reins. An ominous dark shadow rushes downward from above, accompanied by the rumbling sounds of the ground moving with trees crashing and wood splitting. The ground trembles, rumbles, and large boulders and rocks are crashing downward, bouncing and crushing everything in its path. Driven by the instinct to stay alive, Ezra dives forward with his hands, protecting his head as he tumbles and rolls and trying to get out of harm's way.

He lies motionless with his face buried in the cold and muddy ground. The rumbling sound of the earth rushing by no longer surrounds him, and all he hears is the loud inner drumming of his heartbeat, his heavy, raspy breathing, and a high-pitched ring in his ears. Touching the back of his head, he feels the warm bleeding edges of an open wound that causes the pain and ringing in his head.

Fearing that he will probably die if he loses consciousness, Ezra tries to regain control of his mind and body. He had promised his family that he would return, so he struggles to his feet and looks for Shamal and the pack donkey. The tangled piles of rubble and tree branches are too thick and high for him to go back and see if they survived. It is too dark, and sadly, he assumes the worst, that they lay buried under all the rubble. He turns away heartbroken over yet another tragic loss. First the death of his beloved, Princess Andrea, and now, his most trusted companion, Shamal.

The fury of the wind storm is now upon him as he fights for every step and foothold. Remembering the lights he had seen from above, he staggers downward toward the valley floor below, occasionally resting, hoping that soon he will see lights again. Finally, he reaches the bottom, and the trees give way to open ground—making it easier to walk. Unrelenting, the fierce storm continues and now the white rain powder is a misty cloud he had seen in his dream.

"I must be close," he says under his breath and finds new strength to keep going. The howling wind is unyielding, and the clouds appear to be dancing on the ground. He can only see a short distance ahead of him, and step after each laboring step, he trudges ahead by leaning forward into the wind, with his hands protecting his face from the bitter cold.

Thinking of Andrea with her large, brown eyes and long, dark hair distracts him from feeling the piercing wind slicing through his body. He remembers her warm and radiant smile on the day they first met. He knew of her before meeting, but they were not allowed to see each other until they were of marriageable age. She wore a veil over her face that first day, and when she removed it and smiled at him, her radiant beauty and youthful charm sent his head spinning to lofty heights. He could not remember her name and acted awkward unlike a prince. However, he remembers her name now and calls for her, screaming over the screeching and howling winds. "Aaandreeeaaaa!" he cries out, his heart ripped open, exposing it to the bitter emptiness of love lost, and Ezra drops to his knees and calls her name over and over again, whispering, his voice empty of sound, a raspy gargle in his throat sucked dry by the cold wind. "Wait for me, Andrea. Wait for me, my love," he begs, clutching his face with blackened and frozen fingers.

Although very weak, his fear of death urges his feet forward determined to keep going. Making his way through the sparsely covered landscape, looking for shelter from the bitter cold, he feels like sleeping, but again remembers Nubar's warning that if he does, his blood will run cold, and he will never awake.

Will Andrea be there to welcome me into paradise if I die? he wonders. Delirious and struggling to keep his balance and not able to take another step, he slumps to the ground. Reaching around him, he realizes how strange the ground feels. It is as flat and smooth as a marble floor, but the smooth floor is so cold that it pierces his hands like a knife. Not able to walk, he crawls on his hands and knees until rendered useless and numb by blood-chilling needles piercing the flesh of his arms and legs.

Keeping his eyes nearly closed, he tries hard to see through the white cloud dust swirling around him like a desert sandstorm. Silhouettes of tall trees are scattered against the hillside, encircling him and the large marble floor as far as he could see. The faint images of the landscape encircling him remind him again of the strange dream he had that promised peace and an end to his heartfelt pain and misery. He leans backward with his legs folded under him, so weak that he cannot straighten them. With the back of his head resting on the hard surface, he rolls over on his side to take one last look. He notices a dark shadow moving toward him from the outer rim of the smooth marble floor. Then a gust of wind stirs up more cloud dust, and the shadow disappears. He dismisses it as a mirage like those he has seen in the desert playing tricks on one's mind. No longer able to keep his eyes open, he apologizes to his mother for not returning as he promised as if she is kneeling by his side. Then strangely, as he gives in to death, a sense of warmth and peacefulness overcomes him. He no longer feels his weight on the cold, marble-like ground. He feels as though he is floating in air and no longer shredded apart by the slicing wind. He closes his eyes, calling out to his princess, and drifts off to a timeless place between life and death. In this state of nothingness, the howling wind is silent, and he drifts into an emptiness where dreams are not of this world, but of brilliant streams of light inviting him out of the darkness and where time stands still.

Somewhere in the recesses of his mind, he hears his mother calling to him and his father encouraging him not to give up the fight and live. Images of the last few days at home in their palace flicker on, then off. In them, Nicholas and Nubar test his knowledge of language, his father King Caspar, a wise man who had also studied the stars, testing his knowledge of the heavens. The dazzling lights disappear and the images appear more lucid of the day he departed as his younger brother Isaiah waves good-bye and warns him to stay away from belly dancers, and his sister Vera waving good-bye while brushing tears from her eyes at the same moment he brushes tears from his. Then, darkness fills his mind's eye once again.

He realizes his body is no longer on a cold, hard surface, but instead, something warm and soft is beneath him and wraps him like a soft blanket.

"I'm alive, but why can't I see … why can't I open my eyes?" he asks … awake in the dark corners of his mind. In his dreamlike state, Ezra attempts to take control of his body.

"Reach up and touch my face!" he says, urging his hands to move. There is no response. He tries again, but fails.

"I can't move my arms up to my face. I can't feel anything!" Ezra shouts alarmed, struggling to move and escape the darkness of death.

"My mind is awake, but my body is dead! Is this death?" he asks.

"No! No! I can't be dead!" he shouts to himself, but he cannot hear himself speak.

"If I am dead, where's my Princess Andrea?" He wonders, trying to find where he can be, not knowing if he is dead or alive.

He tries calling her name, but his voice does not respond. His tongue cannot move. Then he realizes he is not breathing. He needs air.

"I need air. Breathe!" he orders himself. "I can't be dead. I don't want to die!" he finally confesses and then struggles to awaken.

Gathering every ounce of air in his lungs, he tightens the muscles of his stomach and chest and forces his jaw open, then calls for his princess, "Aaandreeeaaaa!"

Suddenly, he hears his own voice echoing as if in the palatial hallways of his home. He can hear himself breathing, and he opens his eyes into a dimly lit room. The light flickers lazily from a small candle near him. He touches his face, feeling his hands on his face and his face in his hands.

"I'm alive!" he says after taking a deep breath. The air is warm and dry, and he takes another deep breath and exhales. "Aaah! Yes, it's good to be alive," he says with great relief.

As shadows dance in harmony with the flickering candle, he realizes he is in a large cave and has on fresh clothing not belonging to him. His wounds are cleansed and bandaged and his fingers and hands no longer dark and numb. He cannot see the entrance, but rays of light from a small opening highlight the rough stone surface edges encircling a crude barrier. He sees no one in the cave as he moves to gather his legs under him. He calls out to see if anyone will answer, but only the sound of dripping water answers his call, breaking the eerie silence of the cave. His legs are weak as a newborn colt, but after a few attempts to stand and keep his balance, he finally makes it over to the small candle-lit table and braces himself against it.

On the table, he also finds food as if prepared for someone. Once more, he calls out to see if anyone will answer, and once again, only the sound of water droplets echoes in the dark emptiness of the cave. Looking at the food, he recognizes the familiar aroma of bread, thick syrup like honey, and a cup of what looks like hot tea. The smell of freshly baked dough stirs his appetite, and he feverishly eats all of it.

Feeling nourished, he now feels strong enough to move around the cave without stumbling. He looks toward the entrance and moves carefully toward it. Beams of light stream into the dark cave through long strips of bark and old fur pelts woven tightly together, forming a barrier that blocks the entrance of the cave. The barrier hangs from above and swings away as he pushes against it. The bright daylight is blinding, and he retreats into the darkness to regain his vision. Shielding his eyes with his hands, he makes his way around the barrier again. Through his fingers, he can see that the storm has subsided, but has covered everything with a thick layer of cloud dust. Tree branches hang low with the weight of the dust held in its branches.

"This indeed is strange, but it's the place of my dreams, and at long last in this beautiful place, I'm calm and untroubled with the loss of my dear Princess Andrea," he says with a clear sense that his pain and misery has left him. It now seems certain he has another chance to find peace and happiness.

CHAPTER II

The Cave Dweller Princess

For several hours, Ezra sits and waits outside the entrance of the cave, hoping someone will return. Soon it will turn dark, and the air is cold enough that he can see the warm air of his breath mist in the approaching night air. Retreating into the cave, Ezra hopes to start a fire, and after his eyes adjust to the dimness of the cave, he notices three flickering candles burning instead of just one. His eyes scan the far corners from one side to the other to see if someone is in the cave with him. Checking behind him as he moves forward deeper into the cave, Ezra turns just in time to see the barrier swing shut as if someone rushed out. He runs back to the entrance to get a glimpse of what moved the barrier, but he is too late. The fading light of the evening gave cover for whoever ran out of the opening, and Ezra's legs are still too weak to give chase.

"If it was really someone, why did that person leave?" He asks himself, puzzled, then looks back toward the table with three candles and is surprised to see that more food has been left.

Returning to the table once again, he finds a cup of tea made of fresh, green, mint-scented leaves. Another cup is full with an assortment of roasted nuts and dried berries. Remembering he wanted to build a fire to keep warm, he looks for the fire used to make the tea, but he finds nothing. Strangely, however, it is warmer inside of the cave, though he cannot understand why. With three candles, he is able to see more of the inside walls. Going from one side to the other, he notices that it is slightly warmer as he gets closer to the walls. Spreading the palm of his hand to touch the wall, it feels warm and soothing, and dulls the icy needles in his chilled bones. He does not understand why it is so, but for now, it serves to protect him from the bitter cold.

Ezra decides to search as much of the cave as possible. While holding a candle, he walks toward the far dark corner. There he finds entrances to other rooms, but no back entrance going out of the cave. He wonders how someone would have gotten in without being noticed, or if that person had been there all along in one of the rooms.

One of the rooms looks well kept. It is clean, and the bedding and rugs are neat and straight as his mother insisted their servants do in their rooms. It is decorative with fine, handmade ornaments, and the air is fragrant like spring blossoms. The other room is in disarray, like the living area of their stable workers near the palace, and smells of old bedding and hay. The last room is different. It looks like a meeting area or a place of worship with a raised stone platform and steps in the center of the room, and also a stone altar centered on the top platform. The flat stone altar is unlike any he has seen, having a gemlike quality that reflects the flickering candlelight. The altar sits on a dark fur rug large enough to cover the entire top platform, displaying the altar as a precious gem placed on fine cloth to preserve its beauty. He moves up the steps cautiously and across the platform to the center. He feels the fur rug giving way under each step in his soft leather boots.

On the table, Ezra notices a simple but finely crafted and polished wooden box with shiny metallic latches holding its cover closed. He thinks of picking it up to admire its exquisite quality and wonders how making it is possible in such crude surroundings. He reaches out to touch it but jolts back startled when a spark jumps from the metallic latch to his finger. It's a warning not to touch anything, says an inner voice. Stepping off the platform, he notices images of a strange animal etched on the walls of the room. With eyes focused and furrowed brow, he examines the drawings carefully, tracing the images with his fingers, and determines that it is of the animal he has heard of with tree branches growing out of its head, called a reindeer. The reindeer are drawn standing and running, and they appear to be flying toward the stars and moon that are etched onto the walls. He recalls Nubar telling him of similar drawings he found while traveling and told of ancient legends and beliefs about the reindeer.

He is curious to know where the food came from and continues his search, looking for a storage area. There is none. *It's very strange indeed, but at the very least, I know where there is water,* he thinks. He turns toward a corner where a pool forms from water dripping down the wall.

Returning to the table to enjoy the morsels of food left for him, Ezra continues talking to himself, now feeling more comfortable in his surroundings. "It's strange, but I feel as though I belong here," he says.

The next morning, Ezra awakes, feeling well rested. He looks toward the table and is startled by someone sitting and smiling at him. "Hah!" Ezra yelps, his face contorted, with eyes and mouth wide open.

Smiling back, the stranger replies, "Hello also…. How do you feel this morning? Do you understand me?"

"Yes, you speak the nomadic language of the north," replies Ezra, surprised, and then he continues. "Who are you, and where am I?" he asks and feels more relaxed after hearing a familiar language spoken.

"My name is Herald. And are you a prince?" the stranger asks, still smiling, waiting for Ezra to agree.

"How is it you know that I'm a prince?" he asks, surprised by what the stranger knows of him.

"I know you're a prince, but I don't know your name," says Herald with pouting lips and eyebrows frowning in curiosity.

"I'm Ezra, son of King Caspar of a kingdom in Arabia. But again, I ask you, please, tell me, how is it you know I'm a prince?" he asks again with a puzzled look on his face.

"In time I will tell you, Prince Ezra. For now, it's important you receive more nourishment and gain strength," says Herald.

Ezra is accustomed to having his questions answered. Being a little impatient, he wants Herald to tell how he knows that he is a prince. "Tell me then, Herald. Where am I? And how long have I been in this cave?"

"You are here, Prince Ezra, where you're supposed to be, at Star Lake, and you've slept now for three days in this cave. Do you have any more questions, Prince Ezra?" he asks.

"Where I'm supposed to be?" Ezra repeats confused, and grows uneasy with Herald's mysteriousness.

"Yes, did you not dream of this place and then left your home in search of it?" asks Herald.

"Yes, Herald, but how do you know of this?" asks the prince, becoming more confused.

"You spoke of it while you were asleep, Prince Ezra."

Ezra's confused expression disappears, and he feels for the moment, to be contented. "I have many questions. This is all so strange. Please, if you would oblige me and answer them, I may be able to rest easier," he pleads, trying not to sound frustrated.

Herald agrees. "Well then, Prince, ask away."

"Herald, tell me, who lives here with you?"

"No one lives here with me, Prince Ezra."

"Then who lives in the other two rooms, one of which is neat and clean?" Ezra asks, pointing to the rear of the cave.

"Oh, I'm sorry, I forgot. Hannah uses that room," says Herald.

"Hannah, so who is Hannah?" he asks, now more curious than ever after realizing the person occupying the room is a woman.

There is a long pause as if Herald is thinking carefully of what he will say. "Well, Hannah is my sister. Yes, she's my sister," he says, smiling.

Ezra finds his manner of answering very strange, as if Herald is keeping the truth from him.

Continuing, Herald explains that she actually lives in Tobolsk, but as a young girl, she used to come here often to visit and play in the cave. "This is her secret castle where she pretends to live as a princess," Herald explains.

"Why don't you live in the town also?" Ezra asks.

"Most of the people think I'm strange because of stories I tell the children. I don't care to visit or spend time with most of them, and I'm much happier here with Boris and the reindeer."

"Who is Boris?" Ezra asks, more relaxed, and enjoying the conversation he is now having with Herald.

"Boris sleeps in the other room, and you are lucky you didn't wake him from his long winter sleep," says Herald.

Ezra seems confused again. "What do you mean by long winter sleep, Herald?"

"Winter is the season that is now starting. It gets very cold as you discovered, and animals like the bear sleep through the winter."

"But what about Boris, why would he need a long winter sleep?" Ezra asks, confused once again by Herald's answer.

Ezra notices Herald's puzzling expression. For a moment, each of them looks at the other.

"Oh, I forgot to tell you" says Herald, and intentionally speaks slower and deliberately so Ezra can understand what he's saying, "Boris, is, a bear."

Upon hearing the word bear, Ezra's heartbeat and breathing stops. He knows what a bear can do to a mere mortal like him. He has seen with his own eyes how ferocious a bear can be. Even the great lion, king of the jungle, is no match for the bear.

His voice just above a whisper, "Boris … is … a bear?" he repeats, not sure to believe him since Herald is so calm.

Once again, Herald calmly nods and adds, "Maybe you mistook Boris as bedding for someone to sleep on, but it's truly a bear named Boris lying on the floor of the other room."

Quickly Ezra glances at his own fur-covered bed and jumps up. Walking backward step by step toward the entrance, he fixes his eyes on the far dark corner to be sure Boris does not awake.

Smiling, Herald calmly watches Ezra retreat, amused that Ezra is so fearful.

As Ezra gets closer to the entrance and turns to run out of the cave, Herald points as if to warn him and then grimaces. He is startled by someone screaming as he turns and bumps into something coming through the entrance. It is too dark, and he cannot see as he stumbles to the floor of the cave.

He regains his footing quickly, knowing now that with all this screaming, Boris will surely awake. He is right; a loud roar comes from the far room as he rushes toward the barrier to push it open and climb the nearest tree. As he pushes, he glances back to see whom he had run in to, and notices someone kneeling, picking up a basket of food dropped on the floor of the cave.

Then like an angel, in a very sweet and calm voice, the person covered by a thick fur wrap pleads, "If you could, please, would you close the entrance so Boris will be calm, and there is no need to be afraid of him."

Ezra lets the crude doorway swing shut, but with his eyes blinded by the daylight, he cannot see who is kneeling on the floor. However, from the sound of the voice, he knows it to be of a young woman.

His eyes adjust quickly to the dim light of the cave, and he walks toward the young woman kneeling, looking for the items dropped from her basket. He notices a loaf of bread close to the wall and stoops over to pick it up. At that very same moment, the young woman also sees it, and both reach for it. "There it is!" they say together. Their fingers touch as they hold on to the loaf of bread. In an instant, her touch stirs feelings within him, and warm blood rushes through his arms and face, as he felt when he first met Andrea. Ezra's eyes trace the soft delicate beauty of her hand, up her arm, then up to a hooded head, but the hood protecting her from the cold also protects her face from his eyes.

Without warning, a deafening loud roar reverberates in the air just above them, and the ground shudders beneath his feet. His heart skips a beat, then quickens as he prepares to run. Taking a deep breath to gather energy, he gathers himself to make a quick dash for the entrance.

Once again, her soft, angelic voice stops him. "Be calm please, and do not move," she warns, as she slowly takes the bread from Ezra's hand, places it in the basket, then looks up at the beast standing on its hind legs towering above them. "I'm safe now, Boris. Go back to sleep, please," she says calmly.

Tilting his eyes upward slowly, Ezra sees the immense creature whose head nearly touches the roof of the cave. He watches in amazement as Boris obeys and drops onto four legs. The ground shudders under its weight, then the beast turns and returns to its room, pausing midstride to look back at him, snarling. It is as though Boris is warning him.

Ezra follows the young woman to the table where Herald is sitting, still grinning as he did when Ezra ran for the entrance. In her shyness, the young woman faces away from Ezra. She removes the food from her basket and tries to salvage what is left.

Herald offers an introduction. "Prince Ezra, although you've already met, unpleasantly it seems, this is Hannah."

Ezra acknowledges with a slight bow and reaches for Hannah's hand. "Hannah, I'm honored to meet you. Please forgive my clumsiness and stupi—" The prince pauses when Hannah runs to her room unexpectedly, appears to hide tears of disappointment, and says nothing.

"What happened? What did I say to offend her?" he asks Herald, looking befuddled.

"I believe she's distressed because this special meal she prepared for you is ruined," he says, while pointing to the food she brought in the basket, which now sits haphazardly on the table.

"But it's not her fault. It was I that didn't look when I ran. I didn't realize why you didn't run also, Herald. I feel like a fool," Ezra explains, hoping Hannah hears him.

Herald stands up and signals Ezra to help him set the table. "Prince Ezra, look at all this food. I'm sure most, if not all of it, is clean enough to eat. We just need to separate what is still clean and put it in its proper place on the table," he says, encouraging Ezra to play along and hoping Hannah is listening.

Knowing Herald is trying to convince Hannah that the accident isn't so grave, Ezra agrees. "Herald, I believe you're right. Let me help you," he says.

Ezra and Herald continue the exchange. "This seems good enough. It looks tasty, too. Should I put it here, or should it go there?" Ezra asks, trying to sound as if the task of setting the table is beyond their abilities.

Herald joins the ploy. "No, no, no, you should know better, Ezra. Meat is always placed on a platter in the center, not next to the bread on the side."

"But I thought you suggested the bread should be in the center," Ezra replies, trying to sound confused.

In her room, Hannah dries her tears and listens to their silliness. She smiles knowing it is just a childish ploy. She could not believe it when Herald told her that the prince for whom they had been waiting has arrived. She still doubted Herald when she agreed to prepare a meal for the prince. However, Herald's excitement had seemed genuine enough to arouse her curiosity. After all, she had waited and rehearsed for this moment in her childhood fantasies of pretending to be a princess.

Now that they are having so much fun at her expense, Hannah decides to retaliate in kind by pretending to be very upset and also very mysterious. She decides to leave her hooded wrap on and pulls the hood tight around her head so she can see out, and they can't see her face clearly.

Walking out from her room, unnoticed, Hannah interrupts their silly bickering. "You can stop your foolishness now, please. Take a seat, Prince Ezra, so you'll not run into me again, and Herald, stop treating me as a child, please. Can't you see I'm a mature woman now?" she says curtly.

Not wanting to appear eager, Prince Ezra waits patiently, admiring her soft, delicate hands as she prepares the table. He wants to see her, but she keeps her face turned away. He thinks of walking around to see her, but remembers Boris's warning and holds his place in the chair. She finishes setting the table, and as quickly as she had entered, she turns away to return to her room. Ezra turns toward Herald who grins and shrugs his shoulders while drumming his fingers on the table.

Ezra tries to stop her. "Hannah, wait!" he calls out. "Won't you join us?"

Hannah pauses slightly, not turning, keeping her back toward Ezra, then says, "I have eaten, thank you," and continues on.

"Please wait," Ezra asks in a softer tone. Hannah pauses again. "It would be an honor to know who is so gracious, so gracious to prepare a meal like this for a stranger and bring it here through the cold wind to this cave. It's a meal and service fit for a king," he says, trying to please Hannah.

At last, the moment is near, and her fur wrap spins softly around her as she turns to face him, and he will see the face to match her angelic voice. Instead, however, Ezra is disappointed when he can't see her through the small opening of the hood. Undaunted, Ezra rises from his chair and moves closer to Hannah, bowing slightly, and gestures openly with his hands that she joins them.

Hannah continues her teasing. "Well, no, you're wrong, Prince Ezra, I did not prepare a meal for a king. I could if I wanted to, but you are just a prince. If not for Herald, I would not have bothered." She turns back toward her room, concealing her smile, knowing they've fallen for her ruse.

As she continues on her way, she announces she will be back to clear the table when they are finished. Ezra looks toward Herald, who once again grins and shrugs his shoulders, then invites Ezra to sit and eat.

Hannah's rejection stings and appears directed toward settling the score for bumping into her. It concerns him when she isn't taken by his charming ways. Ezra offers a reply to her, accepting his status of being just a lowly prince and not a king. "Well, it's certainly a meal fit for this prince anyway," he says giving in to his demise.

There are pieces of roasted fowl, some type of meat wrapped with some kind of skin. Ezra learns from Herald that it's called a sausage, made from another type of large antelope, also with large leafless trees growing out the top of its head—it was called an elk. She brings small loaves of bread, still warm, that he dips in a thick, sweet sauce tasting like sweet plums.

Ezra notices Herald not eating and asks why he doesn't join him. He apologizes for not inviting Herald and offers the plate of sausages. "Pardon my crude manners, Herald. Won't you join me?" he says.

Herald places his hand on the edge of the plate and pushes it back to Ezra smiling. "Thank you, but I don't eat meat, I'm a vegetarian."

"Vegetarian? That's a strange word I've never heard. What is a vegetarian?"

"Vegetarians don't eat meat," Herald says and points to the sausages and roasted pieces of fowl.

He asks Herald why Hannah doesn't want to join them and if it is because of her shyness. Herald says she isn't shy, but maybe nervous, because he's a real prince and not her make-believe Prince Boris.

While he enjoys the meal, Herald tells of how he found Ezra and brought him to the cave.

"I could see that you were injured and dazed. You unknowingly skirted the outer edge of Tobolsk," he explains.

"Tobolsk?" repeats Ezra.

"Yes, it's the name of the village," Herald replies and continues. "I realized you needed help and followed you, fearing you would get lost. And when I found you on the ice, I used my reindeer to pull you into the cave."

Herald describes how water turns hard as rock from the cold of winter, calling it ice, and the frozen rain, snow.

"Indeed, Herald, that is what happened," says Ezra, remembering that he collapsed on a large marble-like floor.

"Are you still heartbroken over your Princess Andrea?" Herald asks with a mournful look, knowing the prince is deeply hurt over her death.

"Did I talk about her also while in my sleep?" Ezra asks, not too surprised by Herald's question.

"Actually no, you were talking to her is more accurate," Herald replies.

Ezra goes on to tell him of the death of his bride-to-be Andrea, about his dream, and how he got there by following a voice from a star.

"I know of that star," says Herald. "All who have entered this Star Lake region have followed that star here. It will always lead you north, and long ago, a large piece of it fell to earth and formed this large valley basin that shelters Tobolsk."

In her room, Hannah listens carefully to what Ezra is saying. While setting the table, she manages to have a good look at the prince who has the physical qualities of a vibrant young man like many of the young men who grew up in Tobolsk, hunting and trapping for fur in the tundra. Ezra appears different. He has a quality unlike any other man. Not even Ivan, to whom she is promised to marry soon. She is deeply touched by Ezra's tender heart and the pain he has endured when Andrea died. Hannah doesn't know that men could possess feelings of tenderness.

Seeing the prince sitting before her, she recalls dreams long forgotten. She has outgrown her childhood fantasies of being a princess and has become a young woman. Now before her very eyes sit a Prince Charming with qualities of tenderness and affection, which she, as a young woman near the age of marriage, finds intriguing and exciting. He has touched her heart in a way she has never experienced and has brought forth emotions she cannot comprehend. She feels confused, nervous, anxious, and she is pulled in both directions. A part of her wants to simply run back to the table and sit close to him, so she can look into his deep green eyes and look at his soul, while she tells him how much she has dreamed of this moment … and the other part of her wanting to be in control of her feelings, more reserved as a princess would be. She knows not be so presumptuous and waits to see how much he will risk in telling her how he feels about her first, and becoming vulnerable to love once again. From her room in the cave, she hears Ezra announce he is done.

"Hannah, words can't describe how much I enjoyed the meal you prepared. Truly, being just a lowly prince, I'm not deserving of such graciousness and generosity. I don't know how I can thank you enough, Hannah," he says, voicing his appreciation so she can hear him.

Putting on her hooded fur wrap that protects her face from his eyes, she returns with quickened steps, acting as though she has waited too long and is too busy to spend more time there. Items on the table find its place in her basket with deft movements of her hands.

Ezra is concerned that she didn't hear his thank-you and says, "I realize you are very disappointed. Is there anything I can do to show you my gratitude?"

"You have done enough," she says, placing an empty wooden platter into her basket and turns to leave, but steals another glance through the opening of the hood.

"Hannah, please, would you stay awhile to visit?" he asks, gently placing his hand on the basket to stop her.

He seems so sincere and genuine that Hannah wishes she has not pretended she needs to leave immediately. "I'm sorry, but I really must return to finish chores at home. My aunt and uncle need help cleaning their stable," she says regretfully.

Ezra senses a softer tone in her voice and once again invites her to stay. He reaches for her hand, holds it tenderly, and pleads, "Hannah, I would be honored if for just a moment, we could get acquainted and make this meeting more memorable."

His gentle touch feels warm and inviting, and her heartbeat quickens. Her heart says one thing, but her spoken words say another. "We have already met, Prince Ezra," she says with a grimaced look, knowing she didn't want to say that. Instead, hoping to encourage him, she squeezes his hand lightly.

The light pressure of her fingers sends a warm summer glow through his body. Ezra is exhilarated and finds humor in her answer. "All I've met of you, Hannah, is a large fur garment that walks, talks, and serves food."

Hannah giggles. Ezra is delighted to hear Hannah laugh softly because of his remark, and he glances over toward Herald for encouragement. Herald gestures with his hands, inviting her to the table where he sits, and moves over to sit on the bed where Ezra had slept.

Hannah can no longer continue her ruse and forces herself to say the words her heart wants her to say. "All right then, but for just a little while," she says, placing her basket on the table, and sits with her fur wrap still on.

The basket blocks his view and Ezra can no longer take the suspense and stands up slowly. "Please, allow me," he says and moves beside her to remove her fur wrap and hood. "Hannah, let me help you with your wrap," he offers, fighting the urge to hurry and approaching her slowly while looking through the small opening of her hood. He can see the reflection of the flickering candlelight in her eyes as they follow the movement of his hands.

She reaches up to stop his hands, unsure if she should let him continue, but his hands feel too strong to resist. She keeps her head motionless while Ezra is undoing the tie on her hood that protected her till this moment. He pulls her hood back slowly while she holds on to his hands, not wanting to let go and not wanting to resist anymore. Her light-brown hair held back from her face falls softly past her blushing cheeks and charmingly pointed chin. The air above her head hints of wild blossoms in spring meadows, bursting sweet colors that tease butterflies and honeybees. Ezra moves back to his chair, but their hands hold on to each other, hinting of not wanting to let go of the moment. He reaches for the basket in front of her and places it on the floor. And now, for the first time, his eyes meet hers.

She tilts her head forward, a habit of her youthful shyness and innocence, and demurely tries to avoid his eyes, and like their hands, their eyes also hold on to each other. Her heartbeat quickens, and her breath shortens. She is unsure of what to say if she can speak at all. But her eyes speak for her, and Ezra's eyes acknowledge. Silently, they speak the language only their hearts understand. The moment is magical, and no one utters a word. It is silent except for the cavernous sound of water dripping into the small pool in the corner of the cave.

The silence is broken by the sound of Herald clearing his throat. "Aharrm! I'm sorry to interrupt your very spirited conversation, but there are things I must discuss with you, Prince Ezra."

"Oh, yes, Herald. There is a lot we need to talk about," remembers Ezra. His eyes still fixed on Hannah and not being attentive to Herald, he speaks to Hannah instead. "Hannah, I would like you to know how truly grateful I am for your hospitality. No one I have met on my journey here has been so generous," says Ezra, being as sincere as he can be.

"Thank you for those kind words, Prince Ezra. But I really must go now. I have chores to finish at my uncle's stable," she says nervously, not remembering the words she had rehearsed to say to the prince.

"Please, forgive me if I'm too bold, Hannah. If you must leave, I must tell you. Your shyness does not conceal your beauty, for you are as beautiful as any queen or princess could be," he says, paying her a compliment and trying to ease her nervousness. "Perhaps, in just a small way, I can repay you by doing your chores at your uncle's stable," offers Ezra, looking for an opportunity to spend more time with her.

Herald clears his throat again, but this time more noticeably. "! If you both can spare me a moment, and before you must leave, Hannah, there is something very important I would like to tell Prince Ezra. Hannah, I would like you to wait for the prince since he offered to help you. After I'm done telling him what he needs to know, he will need the help of your uncle in the next few days."

Herald continues, but now appearing very serious and solemn. "Prince Ezra, I will tell you now of how I knew you are a prince. Long ago, cave dwellers lived in this world knowing only what they could see and touch. They believed the sun, moon, and stars possessed special powers and paid homage to them because the sun warmed the earth by day and the moon and stars lit the skies at night. A bright star of the northern skies was paid special tribute because it guided their way at night. The reindeer was also given special tribute because it provided transportation, food, clothing, fuel for fire, and also their antlers provided building materials for shelter and tools."

"The land was abundant and fruitful, with enough to provide for all who lived here. But the God to whom I pray to, and father to all was disappointed, because warring tribes battled constantly over the rights to gather food and grazing land for their large herds of reindeer. They did not know of the God who had created all that they fought for. So God sent a star to set the land on fire and brought an end to the fighting. All the great reindeer herds perished in the fire except for a few. After a long period of famine, lakes filled, trees grew, and the birds and animals returned except for the large herds of reindeer.

Harmony remained among the tribes for fear of being set on fire again, and they continued to pray for the return of the large reindeer herds. God decided it was time and sent a messenger called an angel to prepare the way for everlasting peace. The angel walked among the cave dwellers and spoke of God's plan for tranquility that included the return of the large reindeer herds. The angel told them that a king of peace would arrive soon, and they should prepare a gift for the king. In the year before the king's birth, a prince from the region of the king's birthplace would arrive in the land of the cave dwellers to take the gift for the newborn king and deliver it to the place of his birth. A star would point the way for the prince and mark the birthplace of the infant king who would be called the Christ child. Thereafter, the season of his birth would be celebrated by all, and it will be called Christmas. I knew by your clothes and the language in which you spoke while you slept; you are that prince."

Thinking of the irony that he, a prince in search of peace would deliver a gift to the king of peace sparks Ezra's interest. "What is the gift made by the cave dwellers?" he asks.

"The gift is strange. It's a finely crafted box made from special wood of a tree near Star Lake struck down by the star. The metal used for the latches came from small fragments of the star that melted in the fire, and reindeer antlers were carved to use as lifting handles and foot pegs. It appears empty of things that you are able to see, but in reality, it holds in safe keeping, solemn promises, and prayers of consolation until it is offered as a gift to the king who will honor it. For many, it was a gift given with their very last breath of life."

"Is it the box in the large room?" Ezra asks, and Herald nods in agreement. "And who is this Christ child to receive this gift?" Ezra continues to ask.

Unsure if Ezra is taking him seriously, Herald replies "Prince Ezra, I can't tell you for sure who this king will be, but the angel told the cave dwellers that it will be a newborn child whose birth will be marked by a new star in the heavens."

Herald continues, hoping it will seem logical and important enough to Ezra. "Prince Ezra, I know not if you believe all I've told you. Most would not. I hope the prediction of your arrival will convince you that God's message from the angel to the cave dwellers about the arrival of a prince is your destiny … part of a divine plan from our God of the heavens who wants us to live in comfort and joy."

Herald's doubts are quickly dismissed when Prince Ezra answers, "Herald, I would consider it a privilege and my predestined duty to deliver the gift. Peace for all is very important, as it was for me when I traveled all this way in search of it," he says, agreeing so Herald will not keep him there longer, and he will not lose the opportunity to spend time with Hannah now.

While his attention is still fixed on Hannah, Ezra asks to leave, hoping Herald will agree. "Herald, if this is all you have to discuss with me, then I would like to leave with Hannah to help with her chores."

Herald can see Ezra is so interested in Hannah that he might not leave Tobolsk before the mountain pass is blocked by snow. "Yes, Prince Ezra, I know you feel indebted to Hannah, but there is one last thing you must consider and why you'll need the help of Hannah's uncle Igor for a horse and supplies. Winter has started, and those not staying must leave before the snow blocks the mountain pass. In a few days, fur traders are leaving Tobolsk. They are gathering supplies now and are getting ready to leave. Perhaps you can join them. While you slept, you spoke of a promise you made to return home. It would be wise of you to do so now to lessen your family's anguish."

"You are wise indeed to warn me of the winter snow, Herald. I must return before the mountain pass is closed. If I'm to deliver the gift, then perhaps you should give it to me now," Ezra suggests.

"I know you are anxious to repay Hannah's favor, so I won't keep you any longer. Please return the night before you leave, and I will give you the box then. I need to tell you other important things that you should know."

Hurrying and not being involved in their discussion, Hannah interrupts, "I'm sorry, Prince Ezra, but I must return now. Thank you so much for your offer to help me. I will let my uncle, Igor, know you will need his help. After you and Herald are done with your discussion, you will find my uncle, Igor, at the stables." Hannah curtly picks up her basket and rises off her chair.

"Wait! Please. I will leave with you now, Hannah. I can finish my discussion with Herald later. Is it all right with you, Herald?" he asks as Hannah turns away heading for the entrance. She pauses to steal a glance at the prince once more, but his eyes capture hers instead and stop her from leaving.

Once again, the moment is silent, and only the dripping water is heard in the cave until Herald breaks the silence. "I can see that there are far more important things you may want to discuss with Hannah. Go now and help Hannah with her chores."

"Thank you, Herald," they both say as their eyes continue to embrace the moment. Then appearing to come out of trance, they both regain their composure and head for the entrance.

Herald watches the prince pull the barrier aside to let Hannah out before him, and he smiles and says, "Prepare ye the way, Prince Ezra. Prepare ye the way".

CHAPTER III

The Prince of Stables

While walking, Ezra finds it difficult not to look at Hannah. He is captivated by her pure and exquisite beauty. Her light brown hair gracefully outlines her heart-shaped face, and her eyes, a sky-colored window, reveal the pureness of her innocence. The tip of her nose turns up slightly, hinting of her innocent youthful charms, and the fullness of her lips curves softly to a smile, with a hint of wanting to be kissed. Ezra is so taken in by her beauty since first seeing her, he now treasures every fleeting glance he takes to look into her eyes and see her smile. Since meeting Hannah, he feels renewed and given another chance at life. Meeting Hannah made him feel like it is meant to be, perhaps part of his destiny yet unfulfilled.

Hannah is delighted and basks in his attention. They walk back slowly, from one side to the other, on the wide banks of the lake, wanting to prolong their time alone. She reminisces about her childhood days, pointing out things of interest, and talks of pretending to be a princess, and about life with her aunt and uncle after her parents died in an avalanche at the mountain pass. For the moment, she stops short of telling Ezra of her prearranged marriage to the son of a wealthy fur trader named Ivan. In her heart, she knows that she doesn't love Ivan, although they have been very close since childhood. She agreed to marry him because it seemed to be the right thing to do. Many other women of Tobolsk envy her. Now, however, after meeting the prince, she knows why she found it hard to tell Ivan she loved him.

In turn, Ezra tells her of his family and what life is like living as a prince in a palace being waited on by servants. However, he keeps his conversation short because he wants to hear her talk instead. Although she has a life full of hardships, he admires her spirit and cheerful outlook. She finds humor in all the hardships she encounters and laughs about it, and her laughter and charm beguile him. She laughs with him also of his stories pretending to be sick so he doesn't have to go to his language lesson, only to get caught by his father, waiting at the stables for him as he tries to sneak out for a ride on his horse Shamal. Now, walking beside him, a woman so beautiful and charming, he finds himself enchanted by her. He had never dreamed that he would meet another woman who could take the place of Andrea, and now he admits that he was wrong.

Reaching the small town of Tobolsk, Hannah offers a smile or a wave to people in the street, but with Ezra, they are stared at instead. Some are puzzled, while others have a look of disapproval. Occasionally, they look back at Ezra, wondering who he is, as he and Hannah make their way to the far side of the town where the stable is located.

Approaching the stable, Hannah points to her uncle Igor working on the anvil near a red-hot kiln spewing out hot ambers from its mouth. "That is my uncle Igor. He is married to my mother's sister, my aunt Ira, and they have taken care of me since my parents died at the mountain pass from an avalanche. I was very young then," Hannah says not appearing to be bothered talking about it. She continues, "Igor is very strong, and he works very hard so he can pay the money he owes Adolph for the stable."

"Adolph? Who is Adolph?" Ezra repeats, trying to keep her talking. "Oh, you'll find out soon enough, but first, let's go meet Igor," Hannah suggests.

Igor was born to be a blacksmith and is known to be the best in the Tobolsk area. He is a quiet, but proud, stout with a strong back and brawny shoulders. It is a perfect physique to take the strain of working with heavy tools, horses, and heavy metals. While shoeing a horse, he can lift and support the horse's weight with their hooves locked between his knees. His callused hands and fingers are strong enough to grab a horse by its nose and lead it around the stable. Igor has a thick beard and mustache, and his face is often smeared with soot from the kiln. But under that gruff exterior, he is a gentle and kind man, and he loves Hannah as his daughter.

Entering the stable, Hannah calls out over the sound of Igor's hammer forming a horseshoe. "Uncle Igor, I'm back."

"Hannah, what took you so long? Don't you know Adolph and Ivan are waiting for their clothes to be washed and their midday meal prepared?" says Igor as he looks up. He immediately notices Ezra, but waits for Hannah to explain why she is late.

"Uncle, if you took the time to check with them, you would know I've already done those chores," she says, then turns toward Ezra and introduces him. "Uncle Igor, this is Prince Ezra from Arabia. He's the one you thought may have fallen off the cliff and was buried with the horse and donkey at the mountain pass."

"Ah, yes, Hannah," he says, surprised. "He is lucky that Herald found him," he adds, then turns to Ezra. "Good to see you're walking and doing well, uh, Prince Ezra, you say?" He is unsure of how Hannah has introduced Ezra.

Ezra steps forward. "Yes Igor, Prince Ezra, son of King Caspar of a kingdom in Arabia. I am pleased to meet you. I'm deeply grateful for the generosity that Hannah has shown to me by sharing some of the food she prepared. I would be honored if you would allow me to repay you by letting me help with some of the chores you have for Hannah," offers Ezra, attempting to persuade Igor of his good intentions, but he fails to notice the worried look on Hannah's face.

"Uncle Igor, I was…"

Igor interrupts Hannah. "No need to explain now, Hannah. Ira and I will speak with you later. Now go and let her know you are home. She needs help packing some of her fur wraps for the traders to take back," says Igor, then he directs his attention toward Ezra. "Now, Prince, where were we? Oh yes, you would be honored you say, to repay Hannah's generosity by doing her chores?" Igor says with a grin and looks toward Hannah slowly backing away.

Hannah gives Ezra a sorrowful look, knowing that her uncle will not make it easy for him.

But Ezra is eager to get to work and answer eagerly, "Yes, Igor, what is it you want me to do?"

Igor takes a moment. He doesn't believe this young man is a prince. Many others tried unsuccessfully to impress Hannah with their claims of riches and palaces in distant lands. Igor is never fooled. He was young once, and he knows the ways of young men looking to win the favor of attractive, naive women.

"Come Ezra, follow me," instructs Igor as he leads Ezra to the small holding pen and stalls where the horses are kept. "I wonder if your eagerness to work would be the same if you knew what Hannah's chores really are. If you are a prince, I fear you may find much displeasure doing her chores. Don't be fooled by her young woman's charms, thinking that she doesn't do what young men her age find difficult to do," warns Igor with a hint of sarcasm.

"Ezra, you can start by cleaning out these stalls, and put fresh hay and water in them. Pile all the dung on the outside of the pen on the far side of the garden. While you're there, fill the wagon with coal for my kiln and pile it neatly next to it. Before putting the horses back into the stalls, check their hooves for rocks or a loose shoe, and brush their coats off with fresh dry hay. Do you know how to work around horses and handle them, Ezra?" he asks, checking to see if Ezra still looks enthusiastic about doing the chores.

"Yes, Igor, I've spent most of my childhood days around horses and our stables at the palace. My father told me that I learned how to ride before I could walk. All I know about horses was taught to me by my father. He, in fact, insisted that I should not have my own horse until I knew how to take care of one properly," says Ezra convincingly.

"Okay, Ezra, you know what to do, but I must warn you about the young black stallion at the end. I have just broken him to take a rope around his neck, but he still has fire in his heart and doesn't know yet to trust men. He belongs to Ivan, Adolph's son. They traded fur for him from a sheik in Arabia and brought him here this summer for me to train," says Igor, as Ezra turns and walks off to begin his chores.

Igor watches Ezra for a few minutes until he is satisfied that Ezra knows what to do and knows his way around horses, then he goes into the house to speak with Hannah about her lengthy absence from home.

"Hannah! Hannah?" Igor calls out wondering where she is.

"I'm here in my room, Uncle," Hannah answers as she quickly steps away from the window. She watches Ezra lead the horses out of the stalls and into the holding pen. It is midday, and Ezra takes off his heavy clothing. She notices his sinewy build through his thin undershirt and is surprised. She assumes a prince will have the less defined muscular features of an aristocrat. Hannah becomes distracted and forgets that she is supposed to help her aunt Ira.

"I'm sorry, Uncle, I needed something from my room, I'll go help Aunt Ira now" says Hannah, as she hurries out of her room.

"Not so fast Hannah." Igor stops her.

Ira looks up from her sewing. "Is anything wrong, Igor?"

"Oh no, Ira, but do you know we have a new stable boy? Since Hannah was so generous in preparing a meal for him, he wanted to repay her by doing her chores," says Igor, with a hint of mockery in his voice.

"A new stable boy?" asks Ira, looking at Igor puzzled.

"Uncle Igor, please!" pleads Hannah, trying to stop him from making fun of Ezra, and also trying to confuse Ira.

"Yes, take a look out the window. It seems the traveler we thought perished in the landslide during the storm is the one Herald found nearly dead at Star Lake. He claims to be a prince from Arabia, Prince Ezra, son of King Caspar, he said. If he is a prince, then I would be Boris the bear," says Igor with skepticism.

Ira gets up to look out the window, and Hannah joins her. "I see him, Igor. My-oh-my, Hannah, who cares whether he is a prince or not, he sure is the best-looking stable boy we've seen around here," Ira says cheerfully, teasing Hannah.

"Isn't he, Aunt Ira? Herald told me that he is the prince the cave dwellers have waited for, and he knows all about life in a palace," says Hannah, hoping they will remember Herald's story.

"Yes, we know of Herald's story, Hannah, but I've told you many times now, it's only a story made up in his mind to entertain the children. You're older now and will soon marry Ivan. You should know better," advises Igor, trying not to hurt her feelings, but wanting her to be realistic.

"I understand, Uncle, I like Ivan, and he is not like his father Adolph. But, Uncle, I'm not sure if I really love him like I should to marry him. We grew up together, and sometimes, I think I love him like a brother," she says for the first time, explaining how she feels about Ivan.

"Hannah dear, when a woman is young, sometimes it's hard to tell the difference between real love for marriage and an attraction not for marriage. I think Ivan is serious about marrying you and is very anxious also," says Ira, trying to reassure Hannah.

"Yes, I know how anxious Ivan is. I think that sometimes he is too anxious. Ever since he has been going with the trappers to their campsite in the tundra, he has changed. Ivan is no longer the sweet, little boy we knew," she says, an attempt to arouse their concern by implying that Ivan has made uninvited advances. But Hannah is disappointed when it falls on deaf ears.

Igor heads out to the stable, grumbling, "Next time, Hannah, Ezra eats the food that we eat, not the food meant for Adolph and Ivan, who pay for it. Now I must get back to work. Adolph wants his new bear trap before he leaves. I don't know how he expects me to make any money if all my time is used doing his work for half of what I should charge him." Igor's voice trails off until the sound of his blacksmith's hammer beat out the sounds of his grumbling.

While peeking out the window for another look, Hannah asks, "Auntie, what can I help you with since Ezra is doing my chores?"

"Oh, Hannah, I know you're not interested in helping me today, but I guess you should, so Igor knows you are keeping busy instead of daydreaming by your window all day. Surely, he doesn't want you out there bothering your Prince Charming." Ira smiles and observes Hannah, noticing for the first time Hannah's fascination for a man.

Hannah blushes, knowing her aunt caught her looking at Ezra. "I guess I shouldn't," she agrees, her lips in a regretful pout.

Outside in the stable, Ezra cleans all the stalls except for the last one with the young stallion. He has taken precautions to prepare the stallion for their encounter by going past the stall on every opportunity, speaking Arabic. The young stallion reminds him of Shamal. It has a strange familiarity in its eyes and its temperament. He wonders if Shamal has also been given another chance like he was given. He can't resist the urge to ask. "Shamal, is it you?" he whispers in Arabic, waiting at the stall's entrance, giving the stallion time to get acquainted to his scent and presence. Cautiously, the young stallion approaches Ezra as if he is also curious. He nods his head with his nostrils slightly flared to test the scent of Ezra.

From the front of the stable where the kiln is located, Igor has been observing Ezra curiously, wondering just who he is. Did Herald use him just to make his stories real? Ezra would have naturally agreed if someone had asked him if he was a prince so he would be treated as one. *Why not? I would do it myself if I needed food and help,* Igor wonders and nods in agreement with him as he watches Ezra.

Heavy footsteps crunching the gravel road fronting the stable warns Igor of men approaching on foot, and he directs his attention toward Adolph and his son Ivan coming through the stable's entrance. *Now what?* He asks himself, as his callused fingers choke the handle of his hammer.

Smiling and appearing friendly, Adolph and Ivan greet Igor. "Igor, have you finished our project yet?" Adolph asks.

"What do you mean our project? You asked me to build your bear trap so you can test it, and if it works, you'll buy more from me to sell to others. I already know it will work because I designed it. I should charge you the full price for this one and sell directly to your trappers," says Igor scornfully. He is still upset over the agreement he made to buy the stable from Adolph. Since making the agreement, he finds that it is difficult to live by it because it gives too much advantage to Adolph, who then uses it to negotiate Hannah's hand in marriage to his son.

Adolph places his hands on Igor's shoulder and reminds him of their agreement. "Now, now, Igor, you're still bitter over our discussion? I thought we had come to a mutual understanding on how we settle your payment for this stable. Don't let this opportunity pass you by," he says, knowing he got the better end of the agreement and needing to convince Igor not to break it.

Adolph is an unscrupulous fur trader who owns many of the trading businesses in Tobolsk. Short in stature and with a protruding stomach that shows his prosperity, he has a reputation for being very shrewd and for willfully using his money to take advantage of people. Many despise him, but can't do anything about it and can only hope that they don't lose too much dealing with him. His son Ivan enjoys the spoils of his father's success and is easily influenced and intimidated by his father's unruly misdemeanor. Soon Ivan will be of age for marriage and will have Hannah for his bride. It is an arrangement agreed on between Igor and Adolph. Ivan doesn't enjoy the life as a fur trapper living in the tundra. Although his father wishes he would manage the northern campsite where most of their trappers live in the summer, Ivan prefers to live in the larger towns where they sell their furs.

Ivan notices Ezra walking the black Arabian stallion out from the stalls and into the holding pen. "Igor, who is that stranger leading my horse out of the stall?"

Igor turns to look. Not because he doesn't know who it is, but because he didn't think Ezra had the courage to walk into the stall and put a rope around the horse's neck. More surprisingly, the stallion isn't rearing up to fight the rope, but keeps the rope slack following Ezra. Igor can't believe what he is seeing but answers Ivan. "Oh yes, that's Ezra, my new stable boy. He's the traveler we thought was forced off the cliff by the landslide at the pass the night of the storm," says Igor, still a little bewildered.

"So, he's the one the townspeople speak of that Hannah brought back from Herald's cave," says Adolph, as he curiously looks at Ezra.

Ivan comments, "It appears he's very skillful in handling the young stallion."

"Maybe you can learn something from him, Ivan, and not use your father's cruel methods," suggests Igor with sarcasm, knowing Ivan wished he had as much success with the horse.

"Where is he from, Igor?" ask Ivan.

"He claims to be from Arabia, a prince, son of a king named Caspar," answer Igor.

Adolph sneers. "I think he worked in the king's stables instead." Ivan laughs with Igor who gives an obligatory chuckle.

Adolph directs his attention to Igor. "Come, Igor, I would like to meet your new stable boy. Maybe he can do a better job of training Ivan's horse than you can. You've had all summer to break him, and now we leave in a week or as soon as my men clear the pass and make it safe," he says, reminding Igor of yet another agreement turned sour between them.

On the way to meet Ezra, Igor grumbles to Adolph about not having enough time because of all the favors he has to do for him. They meet Ezra shoveling dung out of the stall and into a small wagon. "Ezra," calls Igor. "Stop what you're doing for the moment. These men would like to make a business proposition with you."

"Sure, Igor, I'm almost finished. Is there anything else you want done?" Ezra asks, still trying to convince Igor of his eagerness to help.

"No, Ezra, but these men do. This is Adolph and his son Ivan. Ezra, I will give you fair warning, watch how you bargain with Adolph, or you will owe him for your lifetime," he warns Ezra, grumbling, then returns to work on the new bear trap for Adolph.

Ezra notices Igor's mood has worsened since they first met and asks, "Why is Igor so upset, did I do something to displease him?" concerned that he will not be able to ask Igor for supplies to return home.

"Don't be bothered by Igor's squawking. He is upset because he didn't train the stallion to accept a rider as we bargained. But first, tell me, are you really a prince?" Adolph asks.

"Yes, I am. My father is King Caspar of Arabia."

Adolph is not convinced and continues to question. "How is it you know so much about horses?" he asks.

"Because my father insisted that I must know how to care for one before I could have one for my own usage," he explains, wondering where the questions are leading.

"Well, Ezra, how would you like to have the job of training Ivan's horse since Igor doesn't have the time to do it before we leave?"

Ezra suspects Adolph could be luring him into an unfavorable bargaining position since no offer of payment is made. "I already have plans for my spare time, but thank you for your consideration, Adolph," he answers uninterested.

Adolph is surprised. "Why are you not interested?" he asks.

"I promised to help Igor and Hannah in repayment for their generosity in helping me, and I must honor that commitment first. I'm sorry, but would you excuse me now so I can finish my work?" he says, expecting Adolph will want to bargain. He is right.

"Wait, Ezra, I forgot to make an offer for payment. What amount would make it worth your while?"

Ezra decides to push Adolph just a little more, remembering Igor's warning. "Adolph, when must you leave?"

"Maybe in five to seven days," Adolf answers.

Knowing he has the advantage, Ezra asks, "What payment did you offer Igor?"

"Well, Ezra, we never really decided. It depended on how much time he was to spend doing it," suggests Adolph, feeling confident he has the upper hand.

Again, Ezra's reply isn't what Adolph expects. "Very well then, I will ask Igor how much time he would have spent training the horse to take a rider and what amount he intended to charge you. Wait here and I'll be right back."

Once again, Ezra knows his response is not expected, and Adolph is unable to stop him. Walking by Ivan, Ezra looks at him with a slight grin, knowing he showed them they don't intimidate him.

Ivan sneers back, offering his father support. "Father, I don't believe he knows that your shrewd trading skills will outwit his," Ivan suggests, seeing that his father is annoyed with Ezra.

Knowing he has lost the advantage to trade favorably for himself, Adolph scolds Ivan. "Don't be a fool, Ivan. If you were man enough to train your horse, I wouldn't be in this position. Don't assume he is just a stable boy. He could be who he claims to be. The saddle found at the mountain pass on the dead horse had markings reserved for royalty."

Adolph can readily see that Igor found pleasure in hearing what Ezra had to say as Igor glances toward him and grins knowing justice is served.

Ezra returns and makes his offer to him. "Adolph, for the fair value of the new bear traps and supplies for me to make the return journey home, I will train the horse to take a bit in its mouth and follow it."

"You must think I'm a fool. Why just take a bit in his mouth? I need him to take a rider other than you and do as the rider wishes," demands Adolf, assuming its more than what Ezra can deliver.

Ezra pretends to compromise, knowing he has Adolph in just the position he has planned. "All right, Adolph, I will go no further, I will train the horse to take a rider other than myself by the time you must leave. But you must pay Igor gold pieces for his bear trap and the supplies I need, and you'll also give me a horse to ride back to my kingdom. Agreed?" Ezra stares into Adolph's eyes and extends his hand for an agreement.

Adolph hesitates in offering his hand. "That is a high price you are demanding, Ezra, and I see that you leave me no other choice by continuing to raise your fee. I will agree only if the horse is ready to take a rider in four days," he says, then shakes Ezra's hand. He doesn't want to leave the stallion in the stables untrained till he returns, and he doesn't want to pay Igor any more for his upkeep. Caring for a young unbroken stallion on the journey back is too much trouble, and they risk losing it if it breaks free. *Ezra is certainly smart enough to be a prince, but he doesn't know how shrewd and cunning I am in my dealings*, he thinks, as he watches Ezra walk back to clean out the stall.

Ivan interrupts his father's musings. "Father, I will stay to visit with Hannah for a while." Hearing Hannah's name, Ezra pauses midstride, and then continues at a slower pace, curious to hear Adolph's response.

"What for, Ivan? The arrangement is already settled between Igor and I, and I need you to check on the men clearing the mountain pass," orders Adolf, then turns to leave as Ivan follows in his footsteps.

Ezra wonders what Adolph meant about the arrangement. While moving the last cart of horse dung out of the stalls, Ezra glances toward the small window where he can hear Hannah talking with her aunt Ira. He notices the wooden shutters are pulled partially closed so he can no longer see in. It was opened earlier, and he wonders if Hannah is watching him. His heart beats faster from the mere thought that maybe she is looking through the slivered opening. Ezra decides that this is the opportune time to work with the young stallion, hoping she will find his methods interesting and maybe come out to talk with him or watch.

Without wasting any time, he informs Igor of his plan to start working with the stallion and is back out in the holding pen with the horse. He knows of the methods used by the Arabians, and the young stallion seems eager to learn and receive praises from him. With its head held high and long coal-black hair trailing its upturned tail, the young stallion canters gracefully around him. His mind drifts back to his days as a young prince when he wanted to spend every hour at the stables instead of learning languages and customs of other countries. He wanted to be a feared warrior on horseback instead of a noble aristocrat. Glancing at the window from the corner of his eyes, he is surprised to see that his plan worked, and Hannah and her aunt Ira are watching him. It encourages him, and pretending he isn't aware that they are watching, he puts the young stallion through the paces of walking, trotting, cantering, and then stopping, when he pulls gently on the rope. With the young horse standing still, Ezra drops the rope and walks over, whispering words of praises, and gently removes the rope from its neck.

"You make it look so easy, Prince Ezra," comments Hannah from the window.

He turns to face her. "He is young and eager to learn and comes from a noble breed; he wants to be treated with respect and honor. Perhaps if I had something sweet for him to eat as a reward, it would be easier still," he says while petting the neck of the young horse.

"Would some dried berries and nuts do?" Hannah asks.

"That would be perfect, but this is enough for today, I would like to take him on a long walk up to the mountain pass perhaps, and let him use up more of the fire in him. Would you like to show me the way, Hannah? While I'm there, I would also like to know if my saddle and other items I traveled with have been found by the men clearing the pass."

"I would be delighted to, Prince Ezra, I will ask my uncle Igor if we may take two horses," she replies and her eyes light up, knowing that they will spend time together again.

Ezra overhears Hannah ask her aunt Ira, who then directs her to Igor, who, with his mind set on finishing Adolph's bear trap, grunts his approval while trying to bend a curve on a straight iron forming the jaws of the trap.

While on the winding road up to the pass, once again, Ezra is captivated by Hannah's innocent charm. She tells of how she pretends that Boris is a prince, but he will always be too playful and not want to join in on her games. Now that he is grown, he protects her from wolves and other bears, and sometimes from men who are ill tempered when they don't get their way with her.

Time passes by swiftly, and soon they are near the area of the landslide. The sound of men moving large boulders and axes striking tree trunks echo against the valley walls as they get closer. As they come into view, work and conversations stop, and all eyes are on them.

Arriving earlier and not expecting anyone, Ivan is surprised to see Hannah and Ezra. "Hannah, you must have read my mind. I wanted to ask if you would join me on the ride up here."

"Oh no, Ivan, I did not read your mind. Prince Ezra asked me to show him the way, that is all," she says, seeing that Ivan is frowning a little.

"And you, Ezra, or must I call you Prince Ezra? What business do you have with my horse up here?" he says in a gruff manner.

"You may call me what you wish, Ivan, but I'm here with your horse to do as I bargained with your father. How I teach your horse to follow a rope is no business of yours. I'm here because I wanted to know if you have found my maps, star charts, and saddle," he asks, suspecting they did, since the road is nearly cleared.

"We found nothing. You have wasted your time. The wolves took everything as they usually do, and it's also very foolish of you to bring Hannah here without any means to protect yourself from the wolf pack hunting close by. Hannah will return with me, and I advise that you leave immediately before darkness catches you in the shadows of the trees where wolves wait to stalk and attack their prey."

Hannah feels the tension building between them. "Ivan, it's not necessary to be so concerned for my safety, but thank you anyway. I will return with Prince Ezra since it was he who invited me to join him. I know that the wolves will not attack now. Their bellies are full now that they have taken the carcasses. You are making too much of this, Ivan. Come, Prince Ezra, I must get back to help my aunt Ira with supper." Hannah quickly pulls her horse around on the narrow road and heads back without another word.

"So be it," says Ezra and follows.

"But, Hannah, when will we talk of our plans?" Ivan asks, but it falls on deaf ears.

Ezra, however, did hear Ivan, and he wonders what Ivan means. It seems connected to the arrangement Adolph spoke of. While riding back to the stable, he feels uneasy and wants to ask her about what Ivan meant. Not having any siblings, Ezra knew that Hannah wanted to hear more about his sister and brother, Vera and Isaiah. However, she did leave a hopeful clue that the arrangement was just a family matter when she said Ivan was like a brother to her ... but Ezra begins to suspect it is something more.

It is nearly dark when they return to the stable, and Igor greets them at the gate. "I wondered if it was wise for me to let you go. I forgot to warn you about the wolf pack that roams in the area," says Igor.

Hannah snaps back, lighthearted. "Oh, Uncle Igor, you are like Ivan. I knew of the wolf pack before going. They are more afraid of us than we are of them this close to Tobolsk," she says, then adds while riding past Igor who is holding the gate open, "Why do men feel they need to strike fear in the hearts of others to boast of their bravery?"

His eyes roll skyward. "I can see you are learning too much from Ira. Perhaps you should learn more about cooking from her than about men. So be off now and help her with supper, and I will help Ezra put away the horses," he says with a smile, knowing he has gotten the best of her in their verbal joust.

Hannah steps down off her horse. Then with stiff arms and quickened steps, she heads back to the house. Igor chuckles.

"You are much too generous in offering me help, Igor, I can manage to put the horses away myself," says Ezra.

"Oh, yes, I know you don't need my help, but I need to inform you of other things you may not be aware of," he says. "I can see in your eyes that you are attracted to Hannah. I'm not surprised, because most men are," he adds.

"Then why are you concerned?" Ezra asks.

"Because I see the same in her eyes and in her actions…. Did she not tell you that she is to marry Ivan at the end of the next fur season?"

Ezra masks his disappointment and can see Igor's concern that perhaps Hannah didn't tell him. "Why yes, of course, she did. But why must she wait for the end of the next fur season?" he asks, covering up for her.

"I hope by then to have enough to pay Adolph the dowry he asked for. It's our custom here that a dowry is paid by the bride's father before marriage."

"Hannah agrees then with the marriage arrangement?" asked Ezra.

"But of course, Ivan is sought after by many fathers in Tobolsk. I made the best offer to Adolph," he says, thumb pointing back to his chest boastfully. "Besides, Ivan and Hannah have known each other since they were children."

"Yes, I understand, Igor. She did mention that Ivan was like a brother to her. Perhaps she loves Ivan only as a brother, and not as a husband."

Igor looks back sternly and pauses while walking the stallion to its stall. He remembers earlier in the day what Hannah had said about Ivan. "Perhaps it's no concern of yours, Ezra."

"Yes, Igor, you are right. It's no concern of mine." Ezra feels the sting of Igor's remark closing the door to Hannah's heart. "If I am done here, I will go now. I have unfinished business with Herald," says Ezra, with the hope of love fading. Perhaps his being with Hannah isn't his destiny, he thought.

"You don't have to leave, Ezra, you are invited to join us for supper," says Igor.

"You are much too generous, and I thank you, perhaps another night. I promised Herald I would return."

CHAPTER IV

The Cave Dweller's Promise

The walk back to Herald's cave seems longer than he remembers. It isn't as cold as the previous night, but his breath still trails behind him as he makes his way to the entrance of the cave. Not being sure if Boris is still asleep in the cave, he peeks in to see if Herald is in. A single lit candle is on the table, but Herald is not in sight. He pushes aside the barrier, stepping cautiously into the cave, and hears someone's voice. It seems to be coming from the large room of the cave, and he carefully makes his way as his eyes adjust to the light in the cave.

The dark stillness amplifies the steady rhythm of water dripping into the small pool. Then suddenly he realizes that the voice he heard is silent, and he stops in his footsteps. He senses that something is about to happen, and no sooner than finishing the thought, Herald's voice startles him.

"Welcome back, Prince Ezra," greets Herald and notices Ezra's changed demeanor from earlier in the day. "I see that perhaps the work you were so eager to do may have been too much, or was it Igor?"

"Do you mind Herald that I stay with you till I make arrangements to leave?" he asks, ignoring the question.

"Of course not, Prince Ezra, I expected you would, but you seem more interested in leaving than staying. Did you find working for Igor too difficult?"

"Not at all, Herald. I enjoy working with horses, and I also met Adolph and his son Ivan who owns the young stallion. I managed to bargain for supplies and a horse by offering to train the stallion to take a rider."

"Splendid, Prince Ezra, when will they leave?" he asks, interested in knowing how much time he has to convince the prince to do what he is about to ask him.

"Maybe in four or five days," replies Ezra.

"Very well then, we have ample time to talk about the gift you'll deliver."

"But I already agreed to do it, Herald. Is there more?"

"Yes, Prince Ezra. There is much more to this than I had time to tell you earlier today. But first, before I begin, let me ask: Did you enjoy your time with Hannah and her uncle, Igor, and her aunt, Ira?" he says, wanting to know if meeting Igor was a pleasant experience, given Ezra's obvious attraction to Hannah.

"As you could see, Herald, I was delighted to meet Hannah and enjoyed spending the afternoon with her, but I did not have the pleasure of meeting her aunt, Ira. I did, of course, meet her uncle Igor who took the time to tell me of Hannah's plan to marry Ivan, and he made it clear how Hannah felt about Ivan is no concern of mine."

"I see, I know now why you returned looking anxious to leave. Hannah did tell me about the arrangement her uncle Igor made with Adolph. What did she tell you about it?" he asks and invites Ezra to join him at the table.

"She did not really speak about it. She mentioned briefly that Ivan is like a brother to her. However, from what I've seen, I believe Ivan does not feel the same toward Hannah. It bothers me more that she didn't speak of their plans to marry," explains Ezra.

"I would think it's a good sign that she didn't, is it not, Prince Ezra?" suggest Herald.

Ezra ponders the possibilities. "Uhm, you may be right, Herald, but what should I do now that I know? Of course, you know that I am attracted to her, and I have a sense that she may feel the same for me."

Herald gives the question a serious thought. "In matters of the heart between you and Hannah, I'm afraid I couldn't give you advice. But if you are truly in love, have faith in your love for each other, and you'll find that the answer to your question lies within the trust that you have in your love for each other," says Herald, extending his arms to give Ezra an encouraging pat on his shoulders. Ezra's silence acknowledges that Herald's advice is being given a serious consideration.

"Then perhaps you can tell me about the dowry Igor must pay Adolph before Hannah and Ivan can marry?" Ezra asks.

"Oh, yes, the dowry, in my opinion, it's an evil device used by the families of the bride and groom to gain wealth and influence. It doesn't help to foster the love needed in marriage. I'm afraid Igor and Adolph are more concerned about their business arrangement instead of their children's happiness."

"Their business arrangement?" asks Ezra.

"Yes, some time ago, Igor agreed to buy the stable business from Adolph, and I don't believe Igor cleared his debt. Somehow, Adolph has used it against Igor and forced him to agree to the marriage and dowry. I'm sure if you've already met Adolph and traded with him, you must have found him to be cunning."

"But what if a dowry is promised and never paid, then Ivan is not obligated to take Hannah as his wife?"

"That may be so, Prince Ezra, but the consequences would be worse for Hannah, because Adolph can demand to take her as a slave or servant until the debt is paid." Ezra remains silent knowing the hopelessness of Hannah's plight.

"There must be something I can do to help her," he says in desperation.

"Maybe there is a way, Prince Ezra. If you are willing to listen earnestly to what I must tell you about your mission for peace, you may find the answer you search for."

Ezra directs his attention toward Herald. "Then you must tell me. I will listen in earnest to what you'll say," he says, surrendering to the moment, eager for words to keep hope alive and hold open the door to Hannah's heart.

"Then let me begin. While you have agreed to deliver the gift from the cave dwellers to the infant Christ child destined to be king, your mission doesn't end there. When it is time for him to keep his promise to bring comfort and solace to the sick and the poor and consolation to all who asks for it, it will also be your time to give up your life as a prince and return here to live and work, helping the new king prepare the way for everlasting peace."

Ezra's eyes widen in disbelief at what Herald just told him. "That is nonsense, Herald. I cannot give up my life of a prince. I'm destined to be the king of my father's kingdom someday and have prepared my mind and body to be a great king."

"But what about the gift you promised to deliver for the cave dwellers?" Herald asks.

"I will do as I promised to deliver the gift, but no other, Herald," says Ezra, hopeful he doesn't promise more than what he can deliver. He continues, "But, Herald, why did you suggest if I listened to what you said, I could find the answer I'm searching for regarding Hannah?"

"Well, Ezra, if indeed you hope for a chance to seek her heart, then you must return here after delivering the gift, should you not?"

Ezra ponders the possibilities. "Yes, I would want to return if I'm allowed the opportunity by my father. He is eager for me to take over more responsibilities of governing the affairs of the kingdom. But what of the arrangement for Hannah and Ivan?" he asks, wondering if Herald thinks it will present a problem.

Herald isn't concerned and voices his optimism. "What do you make of it, Ezra, from what she has told you? Did she not say she considers Ivan more as a brother and chose not to tell you about their arranged marriage by her uncle and Adolph? Perhaps since meeting you, she has found a reason to hold on to her dreams."

"Do you really think so, Herald? It warms my heart to think so, but there are too many obstacles to overcome in my own life, and to add to it, the arranged marriage and the predicament of Igor. I find it hard to feel there is much to hope for."

"On the contrary Prince Ezra, there is much to hope for. Give it a few days, and maybe you'll find reason to have hope."

"Very well then, Herald, we will speak more about why it's necessary for me to return later to work in service for others, and what I must do to help this new king prepare for everlasting peace. It could be an overwhelming task to take on."

The next day, Ezra completes the stable chores quickly and then starts working with the young stallion. Hearing the snorting and hooves outside her window, Hannah brings out a handful of nuts and dried berries as a treat for the stallion. "Prince Ezra, I hope this will help you, but he already appears to be doing better than yesterday," she says paying him a compliment. Ezra signals the stallion to stop and waits for her to approach him.

"Thank you, Hannah, indeed it will make the job of training him easier." He offers his cupped hand to receive the handful of treats.

Hannah places her clenched hand in his palm, slowly allowing pieces of nuts and dried berries to drop while brushing her fingertips against his palm. "I wish you had joined us for dinner last night. Aunt Ira wanted to meet you," she says. "Will you be taking Ivan's horse for a walk again today?"

"Yes, in about an hour. He'll have worked up a good sweat, and I will have to cool him slowly. Would you like to join me, Hannah?"

"Yes, I would, but my uncle Igor will be concerned if I spend too much time with you, but I have a special place to which I go when I want to be alone. Would you like me to show you this place?"

"Of course, I would, but what about your uncle?"

"Wait for me at the edge of town on the way to Herald's cave, and I will take you there. My uncle will think I'm on an errand for aunt Ira." she quickly turns and returns to the house, knowing Igor could be watching.

As both continue with their chores, they exchange glances and smile when the opportunity presents itself. Ezra senses she is as excited to spend time with him as he with her. The hour passes quickly, and it is time to meet at the outskirts of town. Hannah arrived earlier and greets Ezra.

"Are you ready to see a very special place, where as a young girl, I pretended to be a princess, and Boris was my Prince Charming?"

"I would be delighted, just as long as Boris is not there," Ezra replies, happy to see that Hannah is in a playful mood.

"Oh no, Boris won't be there. I think he has found a princess more beautiful than I," she says and quickly turns in the direction of the lake. "Follow me please, and be careful not to fall and trip over anything," she warns.

"So will I be Boris's replacement?" Ezra asks jokingly as he tries to keep up with her hurried pace. There is no reply, as if his suggestion has fallen on deaf ears, and he fears he has spoken too quickly in trying to give her an opportunity to talk about her engagement to Ivan.

Of course, Hannah hears it and pretends not to hear it. After all, she must not be too anxious, knowing she has been promised to Ivan to repay her uncle's debt. But she smiles as she feels the warmth of his words burn even deeper than the glances they exchanged earlier and continues her hurried pace, forcing him to chase after her.

They reach a small cove along the shoreline of Star Lake. Caused by the oncoming winter cold, the shallow water is hard and smooth like a marble floor and now knows it is ice. Not accustomed to walking at a fast pace in cold air, Ezra finds himself out of breath. He catches up with her and finds her amused at his demise at being out of breath. Not being able to say anything, he bends over to brace his hands on his knees, taking deep breaths. Ezra remembers it being the place where he had given in to death and also where he was released from the pain and anguish of losing his Princess Andrea. Now instead, he embraces the moment and welcomes the chance to find the same feelings of love for another princess before him now, in all her ravishing beauty.

"Prince Ezra, you surprised me, you didn't fall or run into anything," she says teasingly. "Just for that, I'll reward you with some dried berries and nuts while you rest and watch me dance on my palace floor of ice."

"Oh yes, excellent, dried berries, great, dancing" he replies, forced to take a breath of air after every word.

Here at her special place, she allows her childhood fantasies to take over the moment as she acts out being a princess. She sits on a fallen tree to put on a special shoe her uncle had made especially for dancing on ice.

As Ezra watches Hannah act out her dreams of pretending to be a princess again, their eyes meet and hold each other's wishful gaze, and they both know their hearts are not pretending. He imagines how it will be if she returns with him. She will be his princess, and the people of their kingdom will celebrate their wedding. All of them will be invited to watch her dance as she now is dancing for him on the ice, gliding like a bird in flight across the ice of Star Lake, smiling demurely, and using her innocent charms to hold his attention. She finishes her ballet on ice, coming to a slow and graceful stop on one knee, bowing before him, but looking up into his eyes.

"Did that please you, my prince?" she asks.

"There are no words that can describe the beauty and grace of your performance, Princess of Ice Palace," says Ezra and joins her in her castle of ice.

As they enjoy dancing embraced in each other's arms, they both share their love for each other with their eyes speaking the words their heart can hear. Instead of hurrying back, they take a leisurely walk in order to spend more time together alone.

It is increasingly more difficult in the following days to meet secretly without Igor getting suspicious. To discourage Ezra, Igor invites Ivan and Adolph over for supper on several occasions, while an invitation to Ezra is never extended again. For Hannah and Ezra, an occasional meeting by chance is all that they are afforded. Igor keeps her busy collecting supplies for Adolph and Ivan. As Ezra has done for the past two days, he takes the young stallion out for a walk to Hannah's hideaway, hoping she will show up. Before leaving Tobolsk, he wants to ask her to wait for his return. He also considers the possibility of staying instead and delivering the gift for Herald after the winter has passed. Hannah might change her mind about marrying Ivan, he thinks hopefully as he cinches the girth of the saddle tighter. The young stallion bolts slightly, but it is quickly calmed by Ezra's gentle touch and whispering.

Adolph and Ezra agree to meet on the morning of the last day so Ezra can demonstrate the stallion's willingness to be ridden. There is high anticipation for Ezra to make good his promise, and they start early, preparing the young stallion for the trial. Igor is concerned that Ezra doesn't seem worried.

"Ezra, are you sure the horse is ready to take a rider? All I've seen you do so far is to put the saddle on him yesterday. I haven't seen you on his back yet," Igor says.

"Igor, all you claim to not know is what you have not seen. But you don't know what you have seen," Ezra says, intentionally speaking like a wise man to get Igor's full attention. "Worrying would make the horse skittish," he adds.

Confused, Igor asks, "Ezra, what do you mean by that?"

"Igor, you have not seen me on his back yet because I haven't done so intentionally. I maintained his honor by not doing so, in order that others see and cheer his triumph over his own fears of taking a rider. Did you not notice how he did not fear the saddle on his back? Today he is eager to have me sit on his back like he has seen the other horses do. Today is when he becomes worthy to be named and ridden by a prince. From today on, he will be called Shamal. I will name him after the northeast wind that blows strong and steady, a name also shared by a famous stallion bred to serve in the royal stables of many kings."

"I have never heard of such nonsense. You make it sound as if the horse will be proud and honored to be ridden by you," says Igor, sounding very skeptical.

"Not only by me but also by Hannah," Ezra says, knowing that he must convince Igor that the horse is ready.

"Don't be a fool, Ezra; I will not let you take that risk with Hannah," says Igor, now more concerned than ever.

Ezra calmly walks up to Igor and stands directly in front of him, placing both hands on Igor's shoulders. "Igor, look at me. Do you think I am a fool who would really risk Hannah's safety? I know you do not believe I'm a prince, but believe this now, Igor, or that horse will sense your fear and not believe in me also. I can speak to that horse as I speak to you, and we have an understanding about what we must do today. And today, we will both honor each other. I will honor him by giving him a name he can be proud of, and today, he will honor me by allowing me to ride him and do as I want," says Ezra for the first time, speaking in a stern and manly way to Igor, and not as an eager stable boy.

Igor and Ezra exchange a moment of silence, staring at each other. Finally, Igor is convinced. "All right, Ezra, but if anything happens to Hannah, you'll not leave today," Igor warns.

Ezra agrees. "I know, Igor. If anything did happen to Hannah, I would not leave anyway."

"And what do you mean by that?" says Igor, wondering if Hannah and Ezra have spent too much time together and if she has second thoughts of marrying Ivan.

Knowing he could have revealed how he feels about Hannah, Ezra searches for an explanation that will be acceptable. "Igor, why do you worry about everything? I didn't mean anything by that remark except that I would stay and do all her chores until I know she is healthy," he explains.

Next door, Ira bundles and ties a few of the fur coats that she has made for Adolph and Ivan to take with them and sell for her. She calls Hannah to help her secure the cord.

"Hannah, would you please come away from the window and help me tie this last bundle," ask Ira, assuming Hannah is at the window looking out at Ezra.

"I'll be right with you, Aunt Ira. I'm just looking for something in my room to give to Ezra," she answers as she quickly looks in her treasure box for the souvenir she saved for this day.

"What are you giving Ezra?" Ira asks, curious to see what Hannah will give the prince.

"Nothing much, just a small medal I made long ago from pieces of metal I found at Star Lake. It's not much, but I would like to give it to him so he will remember his journey here and the time he spent with us." Hannah approaches, holding the medal up for Ira to see.

"That's nice, Hannah, I'm sure Ezra will like it," agrees Ira. "Now, put your finger here to keep this cord tight, so I can tie a knot," she says while noticing Hannah is not her cheerful self. "You don't want to see Ezra leave, do you, Hannah?"

"Why do you ask me that, Aunt Ira?"

"Because I see it in your face and in the way you walk."

"I didn't know my sadness showed that much. I suppose you are right. These past three days have been like a dream. I know you and Uncle do not believe that he is a prince. It doesn't matter to me if he is or not. I will always remember him as my prince, and I his princess," she says, speaking as if she is still in her dream.

"Hannah, have you forgotten you are promised to Ivan? He is quite concerned you have not spent time with him before he leaves. He has called for you several times while you were at the lake with Ezra and to visit Herald. I understand dear, how exciting it must be to have a handsome young man around, but you must be realistic about the opportunity you have with Ivan. Let these days pass so it will be just a memory for you to cherish when you are old like me. Now, go out there and wait for Ivan to arrive and greet him properly," Ira advises, hoping to subdue Hannah's fantasies of life as a princess.

Outside in the stable, Ivan and Adolph arrive, and Hannah dutifully greets them. They follow Hannah to the pen next to the stalls where Ezra and Igor are waiting for them.

"Good morning, Ezra. Is the horse ready?" Adolph asks.

"He is ready. Are you ready to pay Igor?" Ezra asks in return.

"Don't forget your agreement that the horse will take a rider other than yourself," Adolph reminded Ezra. Adolph has instructed Ivan to pretend not having control of the horse and fall off, thereby canceling Adolph's obligation to pay Igor.

With a serious business expression, Ezra in reply stares directly into Adolph's eyes, warning him. "I have not forgotten our agreement, Adolph. Just don't forget yours."

Hannah watches as Adolph and Ezra exchange verbal jabs, looking for each other's vulnerable spot. She looks at Ivan standing beside her and wonders why he isn't involved since it is his horse. Instead, she notices Ivan sneering as he watches Ezra whisper to the horse in the nomadic tongue of Arabia.

Not knowing what to expect, everyone waits as Ezra continues to talk to the horse at nearly a whisper. Suddenly, as if he has done so many times before, Ezra pulls himself up on the saddle, and the horse bolts slightly but holds its place. Ezra continues to whisper to the horse and reaches over to rub its neck behind the ears. The horse stands calm and holds its head up proud, ears perked up alert, and tail swishing. Ezra turns his attention to all that are watching and makes a proclamation.

"Hear ye all! People of Tobolsk, I present you Shamal, a great stallion. Here after, he will be known only by that name. He's named after the strong northeast wind that crosses over the southern lands of this world." All are amazed as Ezra puts Shamal through the different paces of walking, turning, trotting, cantering, and backing.

Ivan comments so all can hear. "Ezra, you must have used a strong herb to calm the horse."

Ezra is left with no choice but to let Ivan ride Shamal. "Ivan, if you must challenge my integrity, then I will challenge you to ride Shamal. However, the agreement must be honored, and when Hannah rides Shamal as I did, and you fail, it will only be because of your own doing. Do you agree, Ivan?" Ezra suggests, not needing an answer, and turns to Hannah.

Ezra calls Hannah over to the center of the pen where he waits sitting on Shamal. "Hannah, would you like to ride Shamal?"

Adolph interrupts Hannah's answer. "Why do you have Hannah ride first?" Adolph demands an explanation.

"Adolph, our agreement was for a rider other than myself to ride Shamal, isn't that so?" Ezra asks, expecting Adolph's challenge.

"Yes, but that's Ivan's horse, and he should be the first rider," Adolph retorts.

"There was no such requirement in our agreement that Ivan must be the first rider. I wouldn't agree knowing you could easily influence Ivan to mishandle Shamal intentionally so you wouldn't be obligated to pay. You may not believe I am a prince, Adolph, but believe this now, I am not a fool."

Ezra dismounts Shamal and hands the reins to Hannah. "Are you ready, Hannah?" asks Ezra as he moves close to Shamal's head and holds the bit at both sides of Shamal's mouth. He whispers to Shamal once again, telling Shamal of how honorable it is to allow a beautiful princess to ride him. Shamal responds in a way only Ezra understands.

"Hannah, Shamal tells me it will be his pleasure for you to ride him. He knows you have been kind and gentle to him. Here, I will help you get on." Ezra offers Hannah a hand to step up on and lifts her easily so she can pull herself up on the saddle.

Hannah puts Shamal through the same paces as Ezra, but is enjoying it even more. Shamal is high-spirited, showing all the attributes of a proud stallion, but is eager to do the maneuvers asked by Hannah. All the while, Ezra encourages Shamal with praises and applause. Adolph and Ivan are disgusted, knowing not only did Ezra keep his part of the agreement, but he has also outwitted them.

Ezra calls out to Hannah. "That should be enough, Hannah, perhaps Ivan would like to ride Shamal now," suggests Ezra as he helps Hannah dismount, then directs his attention to Adolph.

"You see Adolph, I have lived up to my part of the agreement, I expect that you will also do the same and pay Igor what you owe him before we leave. As for you Ivan, since you're eager to judge my integrity, perhaps you are eager as well to prove you're right. But I feel I must warn you that Shamal will not let you on his back if you are the one who put the whip on him. He remembers and knows who mistreated him," Ezra warns, not wanting Ivan to be injured and to take his warning seriously.

Ivan notices the manner in which Hannah and Ezra exchange glances and is overtaken with jealousy. Over the past days, his jealousy has grown even more with the interest Hannah has shown for Ezra, and now, with Ezra's success at training his horse, his hate has deepened even more. Adding insult to injury, Ezra takes the liberty of naming his horse. Instead of taking Ezra's advice, he's driven more now to prove his virility and horsemanship and demands that Ezra hand over the reins. "Ezra, you speak nonsense, this is an animal whose only purpose is to serve its master. Give me the reins and steady him at the bit while I get on him."

"As you wish," says Ezra, handing over the reins, and moves to the head of Shamal. Holding on to the bit, Ezra glances at Hannah and is surprised to see her delighted that Ivan will ride Shamal. Ezra is momentarily confused and distracted, but quickly redirects his attention on steadying Shamal. Suddenly without warning, Shamal bolts and breaks from Ezra with Ivan half-seated in the saddle. Shamal rears up high on his hind legs, and Ivan is thrown to the ground, falling hard on his head and shoulders. Hannah screams out Ivan's name and runs over to him followed by Igor and Adolph. Ezra runs after Shamal to catch and calm him and take him back to the stall. Returning to find out how badly Ivan is hurt, Ezra can see him still lying on his back on the ground, trying to catch his breath, while trying to speak to Hannah.

Kneeling beside him, Hannah brushes the mud off Ivan's face while Ezra looks over her shoulders and asks, "How is Ivan? Is he badly hurt?"

Upset at Ezra, thinking that he willfully wants to hurt Ivan, Hannah scornfully replies, "Ivan said you let Shamal go intentionally before he was ready. Ezra, how could you do that?"

"But, Hannah, I did no such thing willfully. I'm as concerned for Ivan's safety as you are. That is why I tried to warn him," Ezra explains, hoping she is convinced.

"Your warning only makes it more convenient to have done it willfully, isn't it, Ezra?" Adolph quips.

Ezra tries to convince Hannah otherwise. "I suppose it does sound that way, but I assure you, I didn't willfully hurt Ivan. However, if you insist that I'm responsible, please accept my apology for not being as attentive as I should have been. With you near me, I could have been distracted," replies Ezra, watching Hannah to see if she has heard what he has said and knows what he means.

"What do you mean by being easily distracted, Ezra?" ask Igor, challenging Ezra to expose his feelings for Hannah. He is aware of Ezra's attraction to her, and she to him, and he is not comfortable with it.

"I don't mean anything other than what I said, Igor. I cherish the friendship of you, Ira, and yes, especially Hannah. I am a stranger you hardly know or can trust, and you have treated me with kindness. Your family reminds me of my own, and I think of them often, as I will think of all of you when I am at home," explains Ezra.

Hannah heard and understood everything Ezra said but chose not to show any response. For the moment, she is more concerned about Ivan's well-being. "Ivan, are you able to stand and walk?" she asks, worried his back or neck is broken.

"I'm not sure, Hannah, the fall knocked the breath out of me, and I feel faint. Perhaps I need to lie here for a few moments and catch my breath," says Ivan, enjoying that for the moment Hannah is more attentive to his needs than Ezra's.

"Can I get you water to drink?" she asks Ivan.

"I could use a drink, but must you get it, Hannah? It would be better if you would stay here and shield my eyes from the sun. Perhaps Ezra could get me some water," he suggests, inviting sympathy from Hannah.

"Yes, Ivan, I'll stay if you want. Ezra, would you get Ivan a drink of water?" she asks in a more demanding tone.

"Sure, Hannah, I'll be more than happy to grant him his wish," says Ezra with a tone of sarcasm, feeling the sting of Hannah's request. He is suspicious of the extent of Ivan's injuries and wonders if Ivan is just using the accident to his advantage.

"Ivan, don't rush to get up, I've decided we will leave tomorrow instead to be sure you are fit to travel. I've already directed Igor to unpack the horses," says Adolph, leaving to settle his agreement with Igor.

Ezra returns with a cup of water to hear Ivan suggesting that how fortunate it is that it happened to him instead of Hannah, but they stop talking when Ezra approaches. Once again, Ezra feels the sting of Hannah's dissatisfaction for him, with mixed feelings of contempt for Ivan's arrogance. Without expecting any gratitude, Ezra hands the cup of water to Hannah.

"If my services are no longer needed, I will leave you two and help Igor with unpacking the horses," says Ezra as he turns to leave, feeling cast aside. While walking away with his back to them, he finally hears Hannah thank him, but he pretends not to hear.

Ezra finds Igor alone unsaddling the horses. Igor informs him of Adolph's refusal to pay for the trap and supplies because of what has happened to Ivan. Adolph agrees, however, to let Ezra use one of the pack donkeys to ride, if he will take care of Shamal on their return journey.

Igor offers Ezra some consolation. "Ezra, I don't know you well enough to believe what happened to Ivan is an accident. However, I do know you have trained Shamal as you bargained for in my behalf. For that, I am willing to give you supplies for your journey back," he offers, suspecting Ezra is truthful, and Adolph and Ivan once again took advantage of an unfortunate incident.

For the rest of the day, Hannah and Ezra both pretend to be unaware of how they feel for each other. Conversation becomes casual as if they are strangers who just have met. There are times when their eyes meet by chance, but only for a brief moment, as if forbidden. Meaningless conversation follows, then both turn away, and the moment passes unfulfilled till the next.

Late in the afternoon, Ezra leaves to see Herald at the cave to thank him for saving his life and to bid farewell without informing anyone of his intentions. Hannah looks for Ezra to invite him to supper but can't find him. She intends to give Ezra the medal. Not knowing the whereabouts of Ezra, she is concerned that Ezra will not return before going to bed. Occasionally, she looks out to the stables to see if his lantern is lit and only sees the emptiness of the dark night, like the emptiness she feels in her heart.

Finally, she retreats to her room and decides to wait till morning to give Ezra the medal but wonders if she will have the opportunity to do it without Ivan there. Hannah lies awake, not being able to get Ezra out of her mind. She feels that she may have blamed Ezra too quickly at the suggestion of Ivan, and tears fill her eyes as she whispers his name, as if to call him back.

Being very careful not to make any noise, Hannah sneaks out of the house to see if Ezra has returned. She decides to look for him at the cave if he is not in the stables and takes along warm clothing. In a corner close to the kiln where Ezra sleeps to keep warm, Hannah finds Ezra's bed roll not slept on.

Preparing to go out of the cave, she puts her coat on and pulls the hood over her head. She is startled when a hand stops her from doing so, and another hand cups her mouth gently to keep her from screaming. She doesn't struggle, knowing immediately from his gentle touch that it's Ezra. Her heartbeat races as she feels herself being turned around by him, and she brings her arms up slowly to embrace him for the first time. Without speaking, Hannah pulls her head back slowly from his chest and looks up to see his face. It's too dark to see Ezra's eyes, but she knows he is looking deep into her eyes.

The moment seems endless, and finally, Ezra asks her softly, "Why are you out here looking for me, Hannah?"

Captured in a blissful moment of intimacy she has never known, she finds it difficult to answer, but finally, like an angel, she says softly, "Because, my prince, when you leave tomorrow, I want you to know that my heart leaves with you." She tilts her head back, rises up on her toes slightly, and invites Ezra to kiss her. Ezra can no longer resist and is overcome by his feelings of love for her. Hannah embraces him and invites a kiss that is intoxicating and he bows his head to meet her lips with his. They kiss and embrace intimately, and her kiss tells of her desire for him to return, but for now, they both realize that they can't go on. They slowly part and release their embrace. Hannah gives him the medal like the one she wears and tells him how she found two of them and kept this one for this special moment. Then, she slowly turns away to return to her room without saying anything more.

Early the next morning, before sunrise, she hears Igor and Ezra preparing the horses. A moment later, she hears Adolph and Ivan calling to them, and she is glad Ivan doesn't ask for her. She will not be able to conceal her sadness in seeing Ezra leave. She lies quietly in bed, pretending to be asleep in case Ira tries to wake her so she can say good-bye to Ivan. As the sound of horses slowly fades away, her tears fall like rain on a dark and gloomy day, emptying her heart of all the joy and happiness she has experienced with Ezra. It is a lifelong dream fulfilled, but now, just a memory to cherish and endure.

CHAPTER V

Following the Star

Matthew 2: 1-2. Now when Jesus was born in Bethlehem of Judea in the days of Herod the king, behold, there came wise men from the east to Jerusalem, Saying, where is he that is born king of the Jews? For we have seen his star in the east, and have come to worship him.

Arabia Late Fall, 6 BC Year of the Lord

When far-off travelers pass through the kingdom, King Caspar would ask them if they have seen or known of any news of his son. On several of these occasions, he hears of the expected birth of another king in a town called Bethlehem. A wise king, Caspar thinks a journey to Bethlehem offering a gift of goodwill to the new king will be the proper thing to do in order to establish good diplomacy. Concerned the affairs of his kingdom will not be taken care of properly, Caspar has second thoughts of leaving for such a long journey, but his wife, Queen Malana, convinces him that the trip will do both of them some good.

In Caspar's absence and in her role as the queen, she will be preoccupied with teaching their youngest son, Isaiah, how to manage the affairs of the kingdom. It will also lessen their constant worrying over Ezra, knowing that in Caspar's travels he can search for Ezra. She has also heard of the long-awaited birth of the king of the Jews, a king of kings. She thinks maybe Ezra also could have heard of it and would be on his way. Someone of that notoriety should be welcomed properly in any event, and so, she convinces her husband to make the journey to Bethlehem.

On the day of Caspar's departure, he checks with his trusted guide Nubar in the stable yard to see if everything is packed. "Nubar, I was compelled by a spirit in my dreams to bring frankincense as a gift for the new king. Do you have a place to keep this safe during our journey?" Caspar hands Nubar the silver-jeweled case with frankincense.

"With all due respect, my king, you asked that we pack as little as possible to lessen the need for a large caravan. I have done as you requested, and all packs are full and secured on the animals and in the wagons with no room to spare. I will carry this precious gift myself in my saddlebag, but isn't frankincense a gift for a high priest rather than a king?" asks Nubar, concerned the king did not give much thought toward choosing a proper gift.

"You are right, Nubar. However, since noticing that new star in the heavens, I've had the same dream repeatedly that I am to follow that star to Bethlehem and bring a gift of frankincense," replies Caspar.

"So be it, my king. If the new king is not happy with his gift, at the very least, the trip will give us the opportunity to look for Prince Ezra," suggested Nubar.

As he walks toward his horse to pack the gift in his saddlebag, a travel-worn, bearded stranger—who steps off his horse, dusting off his tattered clothing in the king's courtyard—catches his attention, "You there! What business do you have here, and who are you?" demands Nubar, while pointing to the stranger.

"Nubar it is I, Prince Ezra, do you not recognize me?" the stranger replies.

"Prince Ezra? Prince Ezra! It is you, everyone! The prince has returned! Go tell the king and queen!" Nubar announces, walking quickly to greet the prince with open arms.

Ezra has ridden quietly into the yard where the pack animals, men, nervous horses, and supplies are being prepared. The noise and commotion stop when Nubar calls out to the bearded stranger in their midst. Ezra is thinner than when he left, so no one recognized him. King Caspar runs into the crowd gathering around the prince, and they bow their heads, respectfully stepping aside to let him walk through. Caspar is so happy and relieved that he cannot speak. Ezra's demeanor seems peaceful and thoughtful, and he has an easy manner about him. The king knows that his son has found solace. Ezra smiles at his father and hugs him tightly. He does not say much as Nubar and others pat him on his shoulders to welcome him home.

Ezra is surprised to hear of his father's plans to travel to Bethlehem to offer a gift to a newborn king. It must really be my destiny to do what Herald asked me to do, he thinks. The prince takes his father's gift from Nubar's saddlebag and places it in the box from Herald without saying much more about where he had been or how he got the box. "Father, I will explain later, but I must join you on your trip," he says with conviction.

"So be it, my son. We will delay our departure so you will have time to rest and give us time together as a family. Your mother would not allow us to leave otherwise," says Caspar, anxious to hear of why he was to journey with them.

"Thank you, Father, of course I want to visit with the family and it would be good to have a bath, a tasty meal, and a good night's rest. I am sure there will be many questions from all of you, but there is too much to talk about, and it would not give me time to rest. I would prefer telling of the journey after we return from Bethlehem," Ezra suggests. He is not sure what he could tell them without having to reveal his desire to return to Star Lake and seek Hannah's hand in marriage. Furthermore, his father is anxious to have him take a more active role in ruling their kingdom.

King Caspar is disappointed; however, he chooses to be patient and not ask his son. He feels the long journey to Bethlehem will give them time to talk about where he has been. When the time is right, he knows Ezra will share the experiences of his journey, but for now, his safe return has answered their prayers. After surprising the rest of his family, Ezra has a good night's rest, and the caravan departs for Bethlehem the next morning.

After weeks of travel, the caravan is about a half day's ride from Bethlehem when they reach an oasis in the desert just as the day's sun is setting. The oasis is large and is used by many travelers. A grove of scattered palm trees and shrubs surrounds a large pool of fresh water used as a well, and the oasis offers a perfect rest stop outside of Bethlehem. It is twilight, and low in the sky above the distant horizon, they notice a star brighter than any other in the dark and clear desert sky.

They prepare the campsite. While busy giving orders to his men, the king notices Ezra talking with two stately men leading two other caravans side by side into the outer edge of the oasis. He walks toward them. Ezra notices his father approaching and says, "Father, you may find this strange, but they are also on their way to Bethlehem to pay homage to a newborn king," explains Ezra, feeling that it is too much of a coincidence that they have all traveled and met because of the same reason. He recalls what Herald told him, and now, meeting two other wise men with the same purpose as that of his father's, he is certain that Herald's story is perhaps true.

Appearing younger than the other two and beardless with light-colored skin, his father offers to introduce himself first. "I am Caspar, wise man and king from the north, from the area of Arabia."

The shorter of the two strangers, a bearded man with dark skin and hair, offers his introduction next. "I am Melchior, a wise man and also a king myself, from the east, in the Isles of Tarshish."

With a very low and commanding voice, a very tall, very dark-skinned and gray-bearded man is the last to offer his introduction. "I am Balthazar, king and wise man from the south, from the Seba region."

Caspar speaks up again. "Perhaps you also, like me, have been compelled by a strange spirit within to offer the new king a gift of frankincense, a gift of faith, a gift usually given to a high priest."

Melchior speaks up next. "I too have had that same feeling I suppose, to offer a gift, but instead, a gift of myrrh, a gift of hope, a gift for a teacher."

Balthazar looks at the other two and pauses to give thought to what he is about to say. "I find it strange that we all have met here tonight for the same reason, but I find it even stranger what our combination of gifts will represent. I have followed my heart in making this journey and in what I offer as a gift. I am offering three small bags of gold coins, a gift of charity, and a gift for a true king. Together, our gifts combine to offer faith, hope, and charity."

All three wise men nod their heads in agreement.

"I too have a gift," says Prince Ezra. "My gift seems trifle compared to all you have brought, but I was also led by strange events that guided me here and also how I came to possess this gift. I will tell you of this after supper during tea. For now, allow me to place your gifts in this box, with my father's gift. It will be in safekeeping under the watch of my father's guards.

"Truly a wise thing to do," says Balthazar. "Other travelers warned of a band of cutthroat thieves in the area."

"So be it," Melchior agrees.

After carefully setting the gifts in the box, Ezra labors slightly to carry the heavy box to a nearby cart guarded by his father's guards. After handing the box over to the guards, he returns to the side of his father. The three wise men discover that they all studied the stars. As the shadow of night falls over them, they all stand wondering and staring at the star that had beckoned them to follow it, and they talk of its significance and of when it appeared in the sky.

Suddenly without warning, the sound of startled horses and camels breaks the stillness and calm of the desert night. Dark, hooded shadows dart out of the thick shrubs and palm trees, quickly surrounding the three kings and Ezra. Razor-edged swords and sharp metal-tipped lances slice through the air coming quickly to rest on the throats of the kings. It surprises the guards who are unable to move fast enough to defend the kings. Their leader growls out a raspy-throated demand. "Being wise as you say you are, you know that what we want is all your gold and other valuables, or we would be forced to kill you and take it anyway," he says, laughing with a treacherous cackle half coughing and half chuckles.

Caspar identifies himself and pleads for their understanding and mercy. "Before you do anything we may all regret, please hear me out. We are here on a mission of peace. We have traveled from far-off regions you may have never heard of, and we don't have anything of high value except for what we brought to offer as gifts for your new king of the Jews."

"Our king of the Jews?" the hairy, foul-smelling leader of the group shouts. The others laugh.

"We will pay homage to you!" another shouts as they laugh again. "Now hand over your money or die paying homage to no one!"

"Wait!" says Ezra. "We have used up most of our money buying supplies along the way; all we have left with, are our gifts for the king. You may have this box of gifts, but please spare our lives."

The king's guards reach into the wagon. As they lift the box, Ezra stops them. "I will do it myself!"

Knowing the box is too heavy for one man to carry with ease, the guards have quizzical expressions on their faces. To the surprise of the guards, the prince lifts the box effortlessly. Ezra is also surprised because now the weight of the box is much lighter than just a few moments ago. He wonders if someone has removed the gifts from the box. He looks at the guards but realizes it is too late to open the box and check. He offers it to the leader, who more greedy than thoughtful, drops his guard by sticking the point of his sword into the sand and extends both arms to take the box from Ezra. He has seen how easy it is for Ezra to carry it, not expecting it to be too heavy. Ezra places the box on his reaching hands, and to his surprise, the box is too heavy for him to carry. Ezra suddenly pushes the box toward him, and he falls over backward, trapped under the weight of the box.

Ezra is surprised to see that the thief is struggling to push the box off his chest and immediately grabs the sword from the sand, sticking the point of the sword on the throat of the leader. Ezra warns the leader. "Now tell your men to drop their weapons, or you will pay homage to your sword!"

With that, the kings' guards take control of their weapons, and then bind their hands and feet to a tree. With the crisis over, the two caravans of Melchior and Balthazar trek into the large oasis. As they prepare the campsite, Ezra stands at the edge of the oasis, looking at the bright star. *How did that box feel so light with all the gifts still in it, and then become too heavy for the thief to carry?* he wonders. The prince shouts out to the thieves tied to a tree. "How far to Bethlehem?" he asks.

"A short night's journey just over the sand dunes, just follow that star," their leader answers.

"Don't be fooled, son. They may be directing us into another ambush," warns his father Caspar.

Ezra explains to his father. "I believe it's the truth, Father, I too followed a star that led me to peace and the place of my dreams. Let us leave our caravans here and make the journey into Bethlehem tonight. I will tell you of my travels as we go."

"So be it," Melchior agrees.

"Truly a wise thing to do," Balthazar bellows out.

As they travel, the prince tells of how a star led him far north to a cold and strange land of people who speak strange languages, with light-colored skin, golden hair, and eyes colored like the sky.

The prince talks for hours, only stopping to quench his thirst. He tells of how he was lost on a stormy and cold night, not able to see the star that guided him and of the landslide that nearly killed him. He continues to tell them of how Herald saved him and of his experience in the cave with Hannah and Boris. Ezra tells of the cave dwellers and of a visit by an angel who foretold of his arrival and the gift of consolation.

Suddenly, a barking dog off in the distance gets their attention. Looking in that direction, they can see lights from a town over a small sand dune. "There!" The prince points; "Look! The town glows from the light of that star above. It must be Bethlehem."

"My friends," says Balthazar, "let us at least put on our finest garments and enter Bethlehem, prepared to pay homage to this newborn king. I, like Prince Ezra, believe that this star we follow serves a special purpose like the star that took Ezra north. Perhaps when we meet this new king, we will understand. Surely, we will meet some townspeople in Bethlehem, and they can direct us to the newborn king's palace."

As they prepare their garments, they hear bleating sheep nearby and a shepherd calling them. They notice a strange ball of light near the campsite of the shepherd. "What could make a light so bright?" asks the prince. "It's not a campfire but some sort of lantern I've never seen," he adds. Anxious to continue their trek to Bethlehem, Prince Ezra volunteers to investigate. "I'll go ahead and meet with the shepherds to ask if they have heard about the newborn king and where he may be."

"Very well," replies Caspar. "We'll be under way shortly and catch up with you."

Ezra heads toward the hillside where the strange bright light is seen last. It takes a few moments to reach the shepherd's camp, and while approaching it, he notices their hurried preparation, packing belongings in order to leave. He calls out to them and asks them to wait for him. As he gets closer, he realizes that they appear frightened and have huddled together.

"Why do you hasten to leave? I don't mean to bring you any harm," says Ezra.

"We thought you were the angel of God who is returning to punish us for not believing his message. A while ago, the angel appeared to us from a ball of light that came from the heavens. The angel delivered a message that a child is born to become king of the Jews, a boy child, born to a carpenter and his wife resting in a manger. We are leaving now to find the manger," the eldest of the shepherds explains.

"Who is this angel you speak of?" Ezra asks.

"He did not have a name," the shepherd replies.

"Then what did he look like?" Ezra asks, trying to find out more about this ball of light.

"The light was too bright, we could only hear the voice that came from it and said that the Lamb of God waits in a manger," the shepherd explains.

Prince Ezra asks, "Where is this manger the angel spoke of?"

"We were told to follow that star over Bethlehem," the shepherd points. "We must be on our way now. I don't know why we are chosen to receive this special message, but I believe God wants us to watch over his Lamb in the manger."

"Thank you for sharing this special event with me. Like you, three other magi and I also received a message from a star that led us here to deliver gifts to a newborn Christ child destined to be a king. I believe this Lamb of God you speak of is also who we seek. Perhaps we will meet again," Ezra says as he rides off to join the others.

On meeting with his father and the other wise men, the prince shares what the shepherd told him. They look up once again at the star directly over Bethlehem that appears to be getting brighter, and then they direct their attention at each other, waiting for someone to say something.

The prince breaks their silence, "Father, look at the box with the gifts!"

The four metal clasps glitter brightly like the star, and the box appears to have a soft glow from within, like a halo of light.

"The star seems to have a strange effect on the box," the prince continues. "I don't understand why it was so light when I gave it to the thief."

He unties it from the back of the pack donkey. When freed from its rope, the box appears to float for an instant into the hands of the prince. They all stare at the prince as he holds the box on his fingertips as if he was holding a tray of feathers.

"I don't know why this is so. If you need an explanation to calm your nerves, I will offer this," says Ezra. "The star over Bethlehem must have an effect on the weight of this box as the moon has an effect on the tides of the great seas."

"That is so," says Melchior. "I'm wisest of all in the ways our planet, the sun, and the moon affect our life and our seasons. The moon does influence the tides of the great seas at the edge of our world, and yes, perhaps that star may be of the same rock used to make the clasps and cause the box to be lighter."

"Ah yes!" everyone says as they all nod their heads in agreement.

CHAPTER VI

The Search for the Newborn Child

ethlehem 6 BC Late Evening, Twelfth Day in the Year of the Lord They. travel to Bethlehem with the prince leading the way and carrying the box. They follow the main street leading into the center of Bethlehem. From there, they follow a wide stone roadway leading to a palace gate. Looking very stately and kinglike, they are allowed past the guards, and a runner is sent ahead to announce their arrival to King Herod, the tyrant ruler of Bethlehem.

As they arrive at the palace entrance, Balthazar suggests, "Let us only introduce ourselves as wise men and not kings. I hope that King Herod would not be offended or threatened in any way. We are only in search of knowledge and not the spoils of other kingdoms."

"So be it," says Melchior.

Waiting at the entrance of the palace, King Herod, accompanied by his high council and the commander of the guards, approaches them. The high council speaks up first, "Greetings! Who might you be, and to what do we owe this visit?"

Balthazar replies, "I am Balthazar, wise man from the south, in the area of Seba."

Melchior speaks next, "I am Melchior, wise man from the east, in the area of Tarshish."

Last to speak is Caspar. "I am Caspar, wise man from the north, in the area of Arabia, and this is my son Ezra."

Not appearing to be impressed but rather more irritated because he needs sleep at that late hour, King Herod turns to his high council and gives instructions.

"Well, what business brings you here at this late hour?" the high council asks.

For a moment, no one speaks, but all glance at Balthazar. He takes a step forward with head bowed and the palms of his hand clasped together and held to his chest. "We beg your forgiveness, your highness. You humble us with your greatness and willingness to see us at this late hour. Your splendid castle seemed to be where we would find a newborn child that will be king of the Jews. We have come to honor him."

King Herod speaks out for the first time, "King of the Jews? A newborn child you say? Tell me, how is it you know in places far away where you came from that my infant son will be king some day?"

Balthazar senses he should guard his response. "Your highness, many travelers passing through our homeland spread the news of a newborn child that was destined to be king. A king long expected, who was promised by their God to save the people of Israel. Is the child they speak of your son, your highness?"

"Why yes, of course!" King Herod retorts. "I hope my son to be king of Israel someday. Now, how do you wish to pay honor to him? He is asleep at the moment, for he is only a year old." King Herod notices the box held by Ezra and asks, "What treasures do you keep in that box? If it is intended for my son, then bring it forward and show it to me," King Herod demands.

Remembering what the shepherd told him about a child in a manger, but feeling obliged to respond to King Herod in some manner, Ezra is unsure of what to do. "Your highness, we beg your forgiveness if we offend you, however, until we see your son, we won't be sure if your son is the child we seek. Our high council demanded that we be certain by looking for a special mark given to the child by birth."

"Indeed, your highness, we are under strict guidelines," the others agree, hoping Ezra will find a way out of their predicament.

"What mark from birth?" King Herod asks and turns to his high council for advice. "Perhaps then you can simply show us what is in the box," the king suggests.

The prince feels he should at least show what was in the box and steps forward to show the box of gifts. As soon as he extends his arms to offer the box, he stumbles forward from the weight of the box. It suddenly got heavier, and he can barely hold on to it to prevent it from crashing to the floor. He lets it rest on the floor and offers an apology. "My humble apologies, your highness, the box got heavier."

Puzzled by his explanation, Caspar, Melchior, Balthazar, and Herod all repeat. "Got heavier?"

"Y - Yes, heavier." Unsure of what to say, the prince offers a clumsy reply. "H - Heavier, b - because I'm weak from traveling so far without food and rest. Yes, the box seems heavier because I'm weak, your highness," he says, feeling confident it is a reasonable explanation.

Balthazar suspects the box becoming heavier is a sign for caution. He remembers how its weight held the thief to the ground after taking it from Prince Ezra. He realizes that they may have made a mistake and offers a reason to leave while reaching to help the prince lift the box. "Your highness, we are not properly prepared to meet your son, and we should not disturb him at this hour. Perhaps we will stay at an inn to get rested and be more prepared tomorrow so we can pay proper tribute to your son."

"Very well," the high council replies. "To ensure your gifts are in safekeeping, we will hold this box till you return. Thieves who also robbed our shipment of gold to Egypt have robbed travelers in Bethlehem. Soon, our soldiers will capture them and bring them to justice."

"Your highness, it's not our custom to accept such generous hospitality without first offering a gift worthy of your welcome," Balthazar politely turns the offer down.

"Perhaps you are more foolish than wise, Balthazar," King Herod comments. "I'm a king who will not accept no for an answer. I will hold the gifts in safekeeping, and for added security and abiding by your custom, I will invite Ezra to stay at the palace to accompany the gifts. He will keep it in your possession till tomorrow."

Caspar objects, "But, your highness…"

"No more excuses. I am tired and need my rest. Guards, escort them to the inn and take Ezra and the gifts to the guest room in the tower."

Within a few minutes, the guards take Ezra to a room above the ground level of the palace. Through the tower window, he can see his father, Melchior, and Balthazar being escorted out of the town center. He looks up into the dark skies and notices the star still over the horizon. He turns around to look at the box, wondering why it suddenly got too heavy for him to carry. He picks it up again and finds it still heavy, but is able to lift it off the floor.

He remembers what Herald had told him about the gift. It is for a newborn king, an infant Christ child, and King Herod's son is not a newborn. *If he is anything like his father, he will also rule as a tyrant, not a king of harmony and consolation,* he says thoughtfully. He feels his father and the others know King Herod's son is not the intended recipient of their gifts.

Ezra decides that he must escape, but he remembers that guards are posted outside his door. He looks at the window and realizes that while it is large enough for him to go through, it is too high above the ground to jump safely or climb. His journey alone to the north has taught him to be resourceful. He searches around the room to see what he can use, and above his bed, he finds a rope holding up heavy curtains used to keep out the light if one rested during the day. Quickly, he looks down over the window ledge to see how much rope he needs to reach the ground. He realizes that it would be too short to reach and is disappointed. Looking outside again, he notices a tall palm tree below and off to the side of his window and realizes that while hanging on the rope, he can swing to the tree and climb down. Ezra removes the rope and curtains and ties them together. He ties a long, wooden plank taken off his bed on one end, and the other end, ties the gift box. He lifts the box to the window ledge and notices that it is not as heavy as a few moments ago. Once again, the metal clasp shimmers and reflects the light from the star. He blows out the lamps in the room so his silhouette in the window will not reveal his escape.

Without time to question the strange effect the star has on the box; he carefully lowers the box out the window as far as the rope will allow. He checks to see if it will reach the tree and decides to try it. After checking to be sure the wooden piece across the window will not slip, he carefully lowers himself down the length of the rope to the box. While resting his weight on the box, he leans against the rope to start swinging. After swinging side to side at the end of the rope, he is close enough to reach a branch of the tree. At that very moment, the knot around the box slips off. His breath freezes as he feels his weight unsupported, and before he finishes gasping in panic, he realizes the box is still supporting his weight, and he gently floats to the ground.

Suddenly, he hears the sounds of soldiers and horses nearby, and he quickly picks up the box and pauses for just a second, realizing that the box is weightless again and still glowing. He quickly covers it with his neck scarf and looks for a dark corner to hide. The horses are close, and he has no time to think about the strange box. He hides in the dark shadows of the palace walls outside of the guarded gate. While waiting in the shadows, the quiet night suddenly gives way to women screaming and crying in agony. It seems to be coming from all over Bethlehem, some near and some far. He is concerned that something terrible is happening. Ezra hides from the soldiers and waits for them to clear the town center. As he waits, he understands why women are screaming. Soldiers are taking infant children from their mothers and bringing them to the palace. It is not clear to Ezra why Herod is doing this.

After the town center has cleared, he moves from building to building until he is out of town. Remembering the escorted direction in which his father and the other two wise men have taken, he soon approaches an inn that served as a rest stop for weary travelers. He finds his father and the other two wise men exiting the door of the inn and calls out. "Father, it is I, Ezra!"

They are surprised and overjoyed to see him there. "Ezra, what happened? How did you escape?" his father asks.

"Father, you wouldn't believe me if I told you, and I don't know how it happened myself, but right now, there is something terrible happening in this town, and soldiers are taking young infants from their families. We must make haste and leave just in case they have discovered that I escaped," Ezra suggests.

His father informed Ezra of good news. "Son, we were told by the innkeeper that a few weeks ago, he helped a carpenter and his wife who was close to giving birth. He informed us that they were looking for a room, and because the innkeeper did not have any room available and felt sorry for them, he offered the use of his manger to them. He has heard since that she had given birth to a son and should still be resting in the manger. We asked the innkeeper where the manger was, and he pointed in the direction of the star," Caspar says, feeling that there is no time to waste since soldiers could be looking for his son.

Without hesitation, they head out in the direction of the star. Caspar tells Ezra that it will be wise to inform the parents of the child that King Herod will look for them if he hears of their son. Soon, they arrive at a manger, and Ezra recognizes the shepherds he met earlier waiting outside of the manger. They see a young woman cradling an infant in her arms. Alongside her, a man is arranging piles of straw and cloth to form a comfortable bed for the young woman and the infant. The man looks up and notices their arrival. He tells the young woman to wait while he goes out to greet the travelers. "Greetings, I am Joseph, do you need a place to rest? We welcome you to use whatever space is available for you and your animals. The innkeeper has been very generous and allowed us shelter here. Come in, this is my wife Mary and newborn son Jesus. Please, make yourself comfortable. I will prepare tea."

"Greetings, Joseph and Mary," all of them answer.

"We have traveled far in search of a newborn child who will be the king of the Jews," says Balthazar. He points to the star over Bethlehem and says, "We have followed that star to this manger and believe the child we seek is your son Jesus. We are here to honor him and to offer gifts," he proclaims.

Without hesitation, Prince Ezra uncovers the box wrapped in his scarf. The box is still very light, but he places it on the ground at Mary's feet and opens it. Ezra holds up the silver case with the frankincense and offers it to Mary. Caspar speaks first. "I am Caspar, a wise man from the north, from the area of Arabia. I offer your son Jesus a gift of frankincense, a gift of faith," he says graciously as he bows and places the silver vessel at Mary's feet.

Ezra holds out the bronze vessel with myrrh next, and Melchior speaks. "I am Melchior, a wise man from the east, from the area of Tarshish. I offer your son Jesus a gift of myrrh. It is a gift of hope," he says and bows his head low as he places his gift at Mary's feet.

Ezra then presents the three bags of gold coins, and Balthazar takes his gift. "I am Balthazar, a wise man from the south, from the area of Seba. I offer your son Jesus a gift of gold, a gift of charity," he says, bowing graciously and kneeling while placing the bags of gold with the other gifts.

Holding the empty box, Ezra searches for eloquent words to offer his gift. "I am Ezra, son of Caspar, though this finely crafted box seems trifle compared to what has already been offered, I have vowed to deliver this gift from the poor people of the far north who live in caves. This box has been their most valued possession built by generations before them. It is their symbol of peace and is a gift fit for a king, a king of peace. Their story is strange, but since I've made this journey, I find it stranger still how true their words have been."

Joseph and Mary graciously accept the gifts. Then Joseph turns to Ezra and says, "Ezra, I am a carpenter, and I tell you now, your gift is as appreciated and as valued as the others. I have a sense of how much work it took to make it. As you will soon see, Ezra, this gift is truly fit for a king. I was about to gather wood to make a cradle for my son Jesus, but as you can see, this box will make even a better cradle than I could make." With that, Joseph arranges blankets for a cushion in the box, and Mary places the baby Jesus in it. "So, you see, Ezra, it really is a gift fit for a king."

Everyone laughs and smiles with agreement and pleasurable sighs at how comfortable Jesus sleeps while Ezra says, "Indeed it is a gift fit for a king. Now I know what Herald meant, and yet, I know not how in the distant past, they knew of this event."

Balthazar softly calls out to Joseph and whispers in his ear, "Joseph, I fear I must warn you, but I don't want to alarm Mary. We met with King Herod earlier and asked if he had knowledge of the newborn child who would be king of the Jews. Herod claimed that his son will be the king and held Ezra with the gifts to be sure we returned when it was time to present the gifts to his son. By some miracle, Ezra escaped with the gifts. Along the way, he saw King Herod's soldiers gather all male children younger than his own and took them to the palace. I fear you must take your leave now with your family before his soldiers find Jesus. We also must take our leave immediately. At daylight, King Herod will know that Ezra and the gifts are no longer in his palace and will send his soldiers out to look for us."

Joseph agrees, "Yes, Balthazar, I believe your fears are mine also. Earlier this night, an angel from God appeared from the heavens and warned me of King Herod. I will gather our belongings now and make haste."

"One other thing, Joseph," Ezra speaks out while preparing to leave, "the miracle we spoke of which freed me from King Herod's palace, well, I believe the miracle lies within the box. Twice in the past night, it has saved us from harm. Perhaps if you run into danger, think of a way to use the box and perhaps a miracle will happen for you also."

"Ah, yes, Ezra," Joseph answers. "I already believe, and I believe also that this meeting with you is a miracle. I will take your advice. Have a safe journey."

CHAPTER VII

Escaping Herod's Wrath

zra asks the shepherds directions for a way back without going through Bethlehem to avoid Herod's soldiers. They only have a few hours of darkness to be clear of Bethlehem and have a head start. Returning to the oasis is done at a hurried pace, since they believe that the soldiers will know that they should look for them there.

At the break of dawn, they are beyond the hills where they've seen the strange ball of light and the shepherds the evening before. The season is cooler, and traveling during the heat of the day is bearable as they press on. They all agree that King Herod's soldiers will not stop to rest. The soldiers fear the tyranny of Herod more than the desert sun. They will not return without the heads of the wise men and the box of gifts.

It is late afternoon as they crest a hill and see the oasis below. They look back to see if Herod's soldiers are behind them, and on the distant horizon, they detect a trail of dust rising from the desert floor.

Caspar urges them on, "Hurry! Let us not waste any time. I've prepared a plan just in case this happens."

In the oasis, the rushed approach of the wise men alarms everyone in the camp. Ezra is first to enter the oasis and warns them to pack quickly and get ready to leave, then orders all the guards to have their weapons ready, and Caspar joins to lay out his plan. Soon after, they quickly disperse to their own caravans and prepare to defend themselves. They pull down the tents except for one, and campfires were put out except for one near the remaining tent. The thieves on the other side of the oasis are still bound together along with most of the caravan's supplies, servants, and guards.

The towering sand dunes above the oasis cast their dark shadow on the campsite, and soon, darkness will cover the oasis. As the dust settles from the flurry of men, beasts, and carts, the three wise men and two servants sit around the fire near the tent waiting. Caspar looks up at the hilltop where the road leads to the oasis. The bright yellow and deep orange hues of the setting sun outline the ridges of the wind-rippled dunes, and soon, silhouettes of ten soldiers on horseback appear against the golden sky. The soldier at the lead of the patrol points his lance toward the oasis and starts down the hillside with the others following.

Caspar warns the others. "Be calm, as if we do not expect them. Let me do the talking and agree with whatever I say."

Worried, Melchior squeezes between Caspar and Balthazar and agrees, "So be it."

Humored by Melchior's concern for safety and comment, Balthazar quibbles, "Melchior, you indeed are the wisest of the three of us, but surely not the bravest. Have courage, Melchior, I believe Caspar has a good plan. He is the wisest of us in military matters."

Caspar stands up and walks toward the entrance of the oasis. "Remember to be calm, I'll go to the edge of the oasis and act as though I'm expecting Ezra." Facing the setting sun, Caspar shields his eyes while gazing into the shadowed road leading into the oasis. The soldiers approach them as he calls out. "Who goes there? Ezra! Son! Is it you, Ezra?" Caspar says, pretending he can't see who is approaching. He walks up to the soldier at the head and asks, "Is my son Ezra with you, do you know of my son Ezra?"

"Yes, we know of your son and also of you," says the lead soldier. "Your son left the palace before sunrise. King Herod is outraged that you did not return to present the gifts you offered. We have orders to escort you with the gifts back to Bethlehem. If you refuse to go, we are to bring your heads along with the gift."

Caspar walks back toward the others and leads the soldiers into the oasis saying, "I assure you that it won't be necessary to remove our heads. As soon as my son returns, we will leave with you to Bethlehem."

"How did your son escape from the palace?" the lead soldier asks.

Caspar turns and faces the soldier angered, "Escape? Why do you say escape, was he a prisoner? Did not King Herod invite my son as a guest?"

"Well, yes, yes, your son was a guest, but Herod is a king who doesn't like to be disappointed," says the soldier trying to remain in control of the conversation.

Caspar continues to walk calmly while nearing the others, then he turns and asks more defiantly. "Why does Herod want our heads if we refuse to go with you? Why does he fear three wise men?"

The leader is surprised by Caspar's defiance and shouts back furiously, "Why do you question me? King Herod fears no one. I know not why he wants your heads, and I know not why he sends soldiers to slay innocent children, but I do know he will have our heads if we do not obey him."

The leader draws his sword, and his horse lurches forward to Caspar's side as the soldier prepares to strike Caspar. As he raises his sword back above his head, an arrow pierces his forearm. The leader cries out in pain, dropping his sword, and surprised, the other soldiers pull their horses around to see where the arrow came from.

They hear a voice from the dark shadows of the palm trees call out a warning. "Do not raise another sword, or you'll feel the point of an arrow go through your heart."

Ezra steps out of the dark shadows. Along with him, there are four archers with arrows aimed and bows drawn. One archer aims at the lead soldier. Ezra walks over to pick up the dropped sword, looks at the leader, and warns him again. "Do not be foolish to think that because there are only four archers, your soldiers outnumber them. If you so much as breath, it will be your last along with three other soldiers."

He turns to the other soldiers. "Now, which three of you would like to be first?"

The soldiers look at each other and the archers.

Ezra continues his warning, "I ask you again, think of what will be a less painful way to die. By them?" Ezra points to the archers, "Or by them?" Ezra then points to six very tall dark-skinned warriors walking out of the shadows behind the soldiers. They have long double-edged sharpened spears held high above their heads, ready to throw. "Or perhaps them?" Ezra points to eight guards on horseback with lances, shields, and swords, who also emerge from the surrounding shadows of the oasis.

Tension builds as Herod's soldiers turn their horses in circles, looking for a way to escape. Their horses could sense the danger and rear up snorting and fighting the reins that hold them trapped in death's noose that tighten quickly around them.

Caspar speaks out calmly. "Let me introduce myself. I am King Caspar, king from the north region, Arabia. The horsemen are my guards, the best, fiercest, and most loyal of my palace. They are seasoned warriors who will protect my life with their own," says Caspar, looking toward Melchior and encouraging him to introduce himself.

"I am King Melchior, king from the eastern region of Tarshish. The archers are the finest of my guards, who, from two hundred paces can put an arrow between your eyes. The arrowheads are made of tempered iron and will pierce your bronze armor easily," warns Melchior, now feeling bold and brave, then looks up at Balthazar indicating that it is his turn now.

"I am King Balthazar, king from the south region of Seba. The lancers are my guards. These guards are most feared in all of Seba. As a test of their courage, armed with only a spear, each one, alone, has hunted and killed the king of beasts known as the lion. Now, I invite you to test their courage, or would you rather test our tea?"

"Tea?" the soldiers and their leader repeat "Yes, tea." Balthazar raises his cup. "We have come to celebrate and honor a newborn child who will be king of Israel. He will be a king of peace and save the people of Israel. In honor of his birth, we will spare your lives so you can enjoy this special event with your children. As a gift to all of you, we will turn over the thieves who I believe stole Herod's shipment of gold to Egypt. They caught us off guard and tried to rob us as we entered the oasis last sunset. Prince Ezra captured them instead, single-handedly. Our guards found your shipment of gold buried in the sand. My servants tell me that the robbers tried to buy their freedom with the gold. Our people are too loyal to be bribed, and besides, it appeared to be assorted valuables taken from common people. Come, sit with us and tell us of this tyrant King Herod, and we will tell you why we have traveled far to pay homage to an infant child, who will be the king of the Jews."

While Herod's soldiers relax and stories are exchanged, the soldiers of the three kings remain on guard. Herod's soldiers tell of the way the people are overtaxed and why the innocent children were massacred. The wise men are appalled. A message is given to the soldiers to take back to Herod. If Herod continues to pursue the child king, the three kings will return with their legions of fierce warriors and bring him to justice to end his tyranny.

"Herod knows not that we are kings, for we only presented ourselves as wise men. You have seen with your own eyes that we are as we claim," says Caspar. "You'll stay for the night and rest as we do. Our guards will hold your weapons until you are set free and on your way tomorrow. We will leave the robbers tied for you so you may take them back to Herod to appease his anger."

The camp is quiet as they all settle down for a night's rest, preparing for the long journey back to their homeland the next day. The air is cool and helps soothe tired muscles. It is a grueling day for Ezra and worse for the wise men who endured a full day of traveling without much food and rest. The desert sky is filled with stars, and the moon is bright enough to cast shadows on the desert floor. Prince Ezra is alone on the hilltop above the oasis and looks at the star over Bethlehem. How magical it all seems, he thinks, that of the countless number of stars in the sky, two have served to guide him on a journey, a journey of peace for himself, and ending as a journey of peace for the Jews in Bethlehem.

Since meeting Hannah, he thought of her more than Andrea. He is not sure what his mother and father will think if they are told how Hannah has filled the void in his heart. In the last few days with Hannah, he has thought of not returning home. But somehow, he felt that the journey home with the gift was far more important, even more important than the promise he had made to his mother to return.

With his promise of delivering the gift fulfilled, he thinks of returning north to somehow win Hannah's hand in marriage. He reaches for the medal Hannah had given him with a unique design that hangs from his neck close to his heart. She herself wore another one like it. She had found the two similar medals at the lake where fire had melted pieces of the star rock. It was the same metal used for the clasps of the box. With the medal still hanging from his neck, he reaches under his coat and cradles it in the palm of his hands. In the bright moonlit night, he can make out the strange markings on the medal. It looks as though molten metal had formed itself in clay that held together two pieces of sticks that were crossed over the other.

When the metal cooled and ash removed, it held the shape of the sticks crossed over each other. Hannah treasured them as jewelry, hoping someday to offer one as a gift to her prince when he arrived. After a while, she had forgotten she had them, no longer pretending to be a princess and never believing Herald's story of a prince to be true.

The day before leaving Tobolsk, Ezra wanted to ask Hannah to leave with him, but it was too soon. Their time spent together was too short, and it wouldn't be proper. His mother and father will think his love for Hannah is caused only by the emptiness he feels. *How could I convince them otherwise?* He thinks. His father will suggest how it might weaken his relationship with the people of the kingdom, because Hannah is not of the same culture. It will make it difficult for his father to leave the right of the throne to him. His mother will be easier to convince, and might even be happy for him, but he knows that she will never go against his father's wishes, not in matters of the crown. Even if his father gives his approval, Ezra is worried that Hannah will marry before he can return. Half the year would go by before he could travel north.

He looks at the medal once more before putting it back under his coat. He recalls that very moment as if he is still there. He feels as though he has lost control of his thoughts and ability to speak. His heartbeat races out of control, and his blood rushes through his veins like storm-driven waves, endlessly pounding the shoreline. His breath quickens to keep up the pace, and he becomes light-headed as images of his surroundings turn into a swirling blur of dazzling lights. The sweet scent of highland meadows from her hair intoxicates him. His hands tremble as he touches her face, brushing his fingertips lightly against her lips. His arms yearn to embrace her, and his arms reached out on its own. He is powerless in stopping himself. He no longer has a will of his own to resist as their eyes speak of their love silently. It seems like eternity as they embraced each other passionately. He wants so much to kiss her, but he knows that it would not be proper because of her engagement to Ivan, but perhaps, just once, to seal their secret promise of love. And when their lips meet, their fervent passion and desire was overwhelming and uncontrollable. Their intentions to conduct themselves properly were quickly forgotten, but he hears a faint, familiar voice calling.

"Ezra, Ezra! Wake up, son!" Caspar calls out shaking Ezra's shoulder. "The others are preparing to leave. We looked for you for several hours. Why did you choose to rest here, away from the oasis?"

"I'm sorry, Father," he says as he gets up slowly and dusts off the sand. "I came up here to enjoy the cool desert air and to look at the stars. I fell asleep, forgetting where I lay."

"We were all in need of rest, son. Come, let's bid farewell to Melchior and Balthazar. They are ready to depart on their separate ways. Herod's soldiers are already on their way with the robbers. They will report to Herod that they are fortunate to return alive, and that we have divided his gold among the three of us."

"But, Father, the gold appeared to be that which was taken from the people." Ezra is unsure of the need to remind his father.

"Yes, Ezra, you need not remind me, you need to let me finish what I tell you. I will send four of our best and trustworthy guards to the inn. I trust the innkeeper will help them. The guards will be disguised as local people so Herod's soldiers won't know what we'll do. With the help of innkeeper, they will see that what can be returned to the people be done so secretly. Whatever is unclaimed will be given to the innkeeper for being generous and kind to Joseph and his family."

"Ah, yes, Father, you are truly a wise and gracious king," Ezra says, seizing the opportunity to have his father reconsider who the heir would be in case he needs to tell him of Hannah. "No wonder the people in our kingdom respect you so much. Father, I'm not sure I'll be able to be like you. I have much to learn, but I fear that being a gracious and generous king comes from the heart, not something you can teach me. Perhaps you should reconsider who should take over the duties of the crown. Maybe my younger brother is more suited than I."

Caspar looks at Ezra scornfully. "Don't talk foolishly, Ezra, you'll be a great king, I won't have it any other way. Now hurry, Balthazar is old and gets impatient."

Before beginning their long journey home, the three kings and Ezra bid farewell to each other, reflecting on their experiences and how it all happened as though a divine being had planned it. They recall the events and speculate on what it all means. Ezra's chance encounter with Herald and their gift, the star that led him north, the star over Bethlehem that led them to the manger, the angels appearing to the shepherds and Joseph—all being strange and mysterious events leading to one purpose. As wise men, they agree that all that has happened are not random events like stars scattered in the sky. When there is no answer, they surmise it to be how men build courage to believe and build their faith in God.

Caspar is in no hurry to return and waits a full day before starting. It will give the four guards a chance to catch up with them in a few days. The journey home is slow for Ezra. He finds himself thinking more of Hannah each day as his father is preoccupied with writing a journal of all that has happened. Being a wise man, it is important for him that events of significance be recorded as part of the kingdom's history. On occasions, Ezra is called on to add specific details of what happened during their journey to Bethlehem. For a while at least, his father has forgotten about the unfinished story of his travel north.

Within three days, the four guards have caught up with the caravan. They report they have accomplished their tasks without incident. The innkeeper knows of the tax collector who worked for Herod's high council. Herod had taken the tax collector's newborn son also, and in vengeance, he secretly worked with the guards, returning all the gold to the rightful owners and left for Jerusalem. Instead of executing the robbers, Herod had one hand of each of the robbers cut off in the town center to discourage all who would try to steal from him again. However, it didn't frighten the people of Bethlehem who were angered to the brink of a revolt for slaughtering innocent children. His soldiers are too busy keeping order and no longer interested in looking for Jesus.

CHAPTER VIII

A Time of Reflection

The caravan is held over another day to give the four guards much-needed rest. Anticipating Ezra will one day be king; King Caspar takes the time to tell him of duties that would be given to him on his return to the kingdom. However, while the king speaks, Ezra thinks of Hannah. At the appropriate time, to appear as though he is listening, he nods and agrees with his father or asks a question. His father in the meantime is speaking, but appears to be elsewhere in his thoughts also.

Ezra seizes the opportunity to end the lecturing. "Father, what bothers you? You seem to be speaking, but your mind seems elsewhere."

"Yes, Ezra, a very good observation," his father agrees. "I'm worried about your mother and the problems she may be having taking care of the kingdom's affairs."

"Sure father, I understand." Ezra smiles and glances over toward a servant who smiles back. "We know how mother is not capable of taking care of day-to-day activities of the kingdom. Especially since you gaze at the stars all night, recording your observations and theories that you need to spend most of the day sleeping. Are you sure you're worried, or do you simply just miss her close companionship?"

"Umm," Caspar ponders the possibility. "You are much too observant, Ezra. What do you suggest I do about it?"

"Well, Father," Ezra is careful to be respectful in front of the guards and servants. "May I suggest that you could choose one of two options, one being you can go on pretending to be interested in enlightening me on the virtues of good kingship, and I can pretend to be interested without falling asleep."

The servant and guard strain to hold back their laughter. "The other would be to take our freshest horses, two of the strongest guards, one servant, and enough supplies to reach home, and start back today while the four guards rested. You'll travel faster without the caravan and would reach the kingdom days before we do. It would give you much-needed time with mother. She will be pleased and surprised to know that you intentionally returned earlier because you missed her. Also, Father, it would give me the opportunity to be in charge of a caravan and gain valuable experience in the art of being a respected leader. You have schooled me well in using the sun and stars to find my way. I will return the caravan intact, and you'll be proud," suggests Ezra.

"Very well son, very well indeed." Caspar nods his head in agreement. "Your travels afar have matured you beyond my expectation. I will prepare to leave immediately, but I will add one thing to your recommendation."

"What is it, Father?" asks Ezra, anxious and happy that his father is in agreement.

"You must continue to add your observations in the journal I keep of this historic trip. Also, I ask that you write the journal of your journey to the north. Upon returning, we will spend time together as a family in the evenings and hear you tell us of your adventures. What you've told so far, I've found to be very interesting, and I sense you haven't revealed all there is to know. Ezra, I'm proud to have a son like you. Melchior and Balthazar both spoke very highly of you, and both agree that soon you would be ready to take over the duties of the crown. You have proven on this journey to Bethlehem that you possess the courage and wisdom to follow what you believe to be right, even in the face of adversity. I will take my leave now Ezra, so be well."

They embrace; then Caspar turns to his guards and servants and asks them to prepare to leave. Ezra admires the eagerness they have to serve his father and how he treats them as though they were close friends. He loves his father very much and cannot bear the thought of causing him any more disappointment. Ezra wonders about the problem he has brought upon himself. His father will probably tell bits of his story to the family and cause great expectation. He may have already said too much about Herald, Hannah, and Boris when sharing his experience to the magi on their way to Bethlehem. To say any more would reveal how she has filled the void in his heart. It will cause great concern for his father if he has reason to believe that Hannah is to be the next princess bride. Ezra leaves the tent to help select the best horses and gather supplies for his father. At least for a while, Ezra will not have to worry about it. The long journey home will give him time to think of a possible solution.

Ezra takes charge of the caravan without incident. Guards, servants, and guides all respect the authority he is given. He keeps his father's journal current and makes daily entries on their progress. He also remembers his father asking for a journal of his travel north and started it many times, only to drift off in a daydream, thinking of Hannah. He wants to write about

Hannah, but doing so would reveal how much she means to him and how much he wants to return.

Within a few weeks, his family and the families of the guards and servants welcome Ezra at their palace gate. Caspar congratulates Ezra for bringing the caravan home without incident and thanks the servants and guards for helping Ezra. The first night is set aside to relax and spend time with their families.

After supper, Caspar approaches Ezra to ask if he is prepared to share his story. Ezra apologizes for not completing his journal and is cautioned by his father that if he does not make a written record of his journey soon, many important facts will be forgotten. Ezra knows it will be a valuable historical record for their kingdom and tries to offer an explanation of why he has not done it yet. "Father, the truth is, on many occasions I have started to write what I can remember of the journey. When I left here, my thoughts were not on exploring and recording my observations. As you know Father, my heart was filled with grief. As I traveled, I did not notice things I would have if I were on an exploration journey as I've been on before. I know if I were to write something now, it would not be accurate. In the future when the records are used, both you and I may look foolish if the records were found to be wrong."

With his hand rubbing his chin, contemplating Ezra's explanation, Caspar replies, "Umm, son, thank you for your honesty. It would be unwise to make a record of your journey if you couldn't depend on its accuracy in the future. Tell me son, while sharing your experience with the magi, how is it you can remember details of the cave, Herald, Hannah, and Boris, and you can't remember important details while you traveled?"

Ezra grimaces slightly, searching his memory for a logical reason. "Well Father, I don't know for sure why that is so. Perhaps because after I awoke, I was more interested in being alive than dead, and because the experience was so strange, I couldn't help but remember the details of what happened."

Caspar rubs his chin again. "Well, that seems to be a logical explanation. All right, son, for now, let's forgo the need of a journal, and as I promised our family, let's join them in the chambers, and just tell your story as you did the night we reached Bethlehem. Actually, I have already told them some of it, because they couldn't wait for your return and bothered me until I gave in and told them what I knew. I hope you don't mind; we are anxious to know what happened in the three days you spent with Hannah preparing for your journey back home."

As they join the others in the seating room, Ezra feels locked in a dungeon without a way out and no window to see through. He wishes he had the magic box to crawl into and disappear. "I missed all of you so much, and I especially thought of moments like this when we sat together listening to father's tales of adventure," he says greeting the others, while raising his arms to welcome their smiling and eager faces. "I understand that father has already told you most of what happened, there really isn't much more to tell," he says, making a last effort to put off telling them about the time he has spent with Hannah.

"But we don't want to hear just father's version, we want to hear you tell us, especially about those three days you spent with Hannah," pleads his sister Vera.

"Oh yes. Those three days. Well, those three days, let's see now," Ezra stalls, appearing not to remember so easily. "I met Hannah's aunt Ira and Uncle Igor whom she lived with. While there, I helped with the chores in his stable business in return for their generous hospitality. I also met a fur trader named Adolph and his son Ivan who owned a young stallion that I helped Igor train to take a rider. For that, Adolph agreed to take me with him when they left Tobolsk. When it was time, we packed up and left. Nothing more exciting really happened. So really, father, you have told them all that is interesting, so thank you, father, really, thank you."

Caspar rubs his chin, noticing that Ezra appears slightly nervous. When Ezra was younger, he could always sense if Ezra was keeping the truth from him. "Son, if that is all there is, then so be it. Why do you try so hard to convince us of that?"

Just then, his younger brother Isaiah asks Ezra. "Brother, what do you have hanging from your neck? Can I see it?"

Ezra acts as though he has forgotten that he has it on "My neck? Oh, this thing! It's just a souvenir Hannah gave me to take back. In fact, it's for you, here, I told her of my little brother, and she said to give it to you." And he hands it over to Isaiah.

"Look, Father." Isaiah gives it to their father.

"Where did Hannah get this?" he asks, looking at it closely while turning it over in his hands and holding it up to the chandelier lanterns.

"She found it by the lake where the cave dwellers found the melted rocks to make the clasps for the box," Ezra answers. "The design on the medal is left there from sticks that were on the ground when the rock melted. Hannah polished it to keep until…," Ezra stops knowing he is about to reveal his secret.

"Until what, Ezra?" his father asks.

"Un- until Herald found the person who would deliver the gift, and at that time, she also would offer the medal as a gift," Ezra answers.

"Yes, I see, Ezra. Then shouldn't you have offered it also to the newborn child Jesus and not keep it for Isaiah?"

"Yes, I should have, Father, b-but I—" his sister Vera's soft voice interrupts Ezra.

"Ezra, did you bring something back for me also?" asks Vera, feeling rejected.

Ezra lowers his head in shame and answers Vera. "I did not, Vera, and I'm truly sorry. Please, father, forgive me, I have not been truthful. I thought maybe I could keep a secret from you with just a little lie about why I could not write the journal, but it has led to many more lies, and now, I am not pleased with myself and feel ashamed. Vera feels she is less desirable to me as a sister than Isaiah as a brother because of the lies. I love them both equally. Please forgive me."

Caspar acknowledges Ezra's confession. "Ezra, it is wise you didn't wait longer. Some have found out the hard way after lying so much, they find it too shameful to admit what the truth is. Since it only involves our family, why don't you tell us the truth now?"

Ezra agrees. "I will, Father. I have not told you all there is about the time I spent with Hannah. First, I will tell you why I did not write the journal. Father, I did try, and it is true that I was not too observant because of the grief that gripped me. There is not much I can remember accurately. I do remember what happened when I awoke in the cave because my mind was calm and untroubled, and I wanted to be alive.

"She gave me the medal as a gift to remember the brief time we had spent together. Father, I believe she has filled the void in my heart left by Andrea. It is strange, but I feel as though Andrea knew of my pain and sent Hannah to fill the emptiness. I did not want to tell you, Father, because I fear you would think I fell in love with Hannah because of my grief. Although our time together was brief, I feel I have known her all my lifetime. I believe she feels the same also. When she gave me the medal, our eyes spoke the truth of how we felt for each other.

"We did not speak of our feelings. As a payment for the stable business sold by the fur trader to Hannah's Uncle Igor, she had promised to marry Ivan, the son of the rich fur trader Adolph who owns most of the town where Hannah lives. So, you see, Father, a relationship with Hannah beyond what I had is highly unlikely. I don't feel a sense of loss as I did for Andrea, but whenever I started writing the journal, I would simply get lost thinking of Hannah."

"Do you love her as much as Andrea?" Vera asks.

"I think I do Vera, but it wouldn't be wise for me to be hopeful that she feels the same and enough not to marry and wait for me. She feels the need to fulfill her uncle's promise of her marriage. Both her aunt and uncle love her as their own daughter, but they know that they could never offer Hannah a better life with what they have."

Isaiah boldly offers a solution. "Maybe they can't, but you can."

"Thank you, Isaiah. It's not that simple, I wish it were," replies Ezra. "I have a responsibility here in this kingdom to keep with the customs of our culture. It is the duty of our family to uphold our traditions. Not doing so would breed mistrust in our ability to protect our people's customs and beliefs."

"Well spoken, Ezra." Malana nods her head in agreement. "But I'm not sure it's what you wish it to be. However, there is no shame for wishing it to be as simple as Isaiah suggests. Is Hannah happy with the arrangement?"

"I don't think so, Mother. She did not say it exactly, but she didn't seem excited about it," Ezra replies.

"My dear son, Ezra," Malana softly calls for his attention. "If not for keeping with our traditions, what would you do?" she asks.

Ezra repeats his mother's question to be sure he has heard her correctly. "Do you mean mother, what I would do if I didn't need to be concerned over my duty to preserve our people's traditions and customs?"

"Yes, that is what I meant, dear Ezra."

"Why do you ask such a question, Malana?" Caspar interrupts. "Caspar, have you forgotten the circumstances of our meeting?" Malana asks sternly but softly. "Let Ezra answer the question. Go ahead Ezra, what would you do?"

Ezra feels his mother is trying to help him speak from his heart. "Well, mother, it's an interesting question. I would be sure not to make any hasty decisions or plans to avoid placing her in an awkward position. I would return to the northland with a reason other than seeing her just in case she is already married. She may feel she betrayed me if I returned to see her."

"What kind of reason would you use, Ezra?" his father asks.

"I don't know yet, Father, but it must be one that she could believe," Ezra answers.

"Have you told her that I study the stars?" Caspar asks. "If you did, you can return to collect a piece of the star the cave dwellers said fell from the heavens."

Ezra answers with excitement. "Yes father, splendid idea. I believe I did tell her of how you spend many sleepless nights studying the stars. I would collect pieces of the star so you could record your observations."

"So what if she is married, Ezra?" his mother asks. "What would you do then?"

Ezra answers, his enthusiasm toned down. "If she is mother, then it must be so. I will wish her well and return home. I will be sad, but I will know for sure, and she will know also. Our farewell will be one we both must understand and accept."

"What then, Ezra, if she is not married but still promised?" his father asks.

"Then father, if she will allow me to, I will court her."

"But what of her uncle's debt to the fur trader?" his father asks.

"I would offer to repay his debt for him so Hannah is free to make her choice, Father, and be sure they understand that I am not offering to pay the debt as a condition of her hand in marriage." Ezra goes on to explain.

"Very honorable, Ezra," his mother adds. "Then I suggest you offer the payment of his debt as a gift to them from our family for helping you. It would commemorate your journey to Bethlehem and the birth of the infant King Jesus. Let it be a gift that truly in your heart you do not seek for anything in return. If her uncle chooses to invest your gift in some other way and not repay his debt, it will be as he chooses, and you should not feel betrayed. In addition, Ezra, Hannah should not have knowledge of your gift. Knowing of your gift, she may feel that you bought her. So, you see, Ezra, it's not a simple matter."

His father offers more advice. "Ezra, it would be wise to consider if the debt is paid, and she is free to make her choice, that marriage is not discussed. I would like you to invite her here as a guest. She will be free to leave whenever she chooses. Let our family and our people get accustomed to her and her to our people and us. She may not like our climate and our customs."

"You would truly allow her to live here as a guest if she is willing?" Ezra asks, being very excited over the possibilities.

"Yes, Ezra, we would, if it will help you find happiness," his father replies. "Without happiness, you cannot serve the kingdom as a great and noble king. You would become a tyrant like King Herod. Son, you have much to consider about why you would return to the north with hopes of Hannah returning with you. Perhaps it would be wise to spend time searching your heart for what will be right for you and Hannah. For now, let us bid good night and see what tomorrow will bring you."

"Thank you, Father, and you, Mother. Thank you for knowing my heart." Ezra bows, with hands together in deep respect and admiration for his parents and leaves the seating room.

A celebration dinner at the palace is held the second night for all who had traveled together with their families and friends to commemorate the journey. Caspar and his son Prince Ezra entertain the guests by narrating the events of Bethlehem from their journal. Upon hearing of the infant Jesus, and how they were guided by a star and angels from the heavens, they agree among themselves that Jesus was anointed to bring comfort and consolation in the world, and they will call him the Christ child named Jesus. The story captivates everyone, and all feel a sense of tranquility. For those who had made the trip, it is a feeling of accomplishment—serving a higher purpose than their own. Everyone enjoys the evening so much; King Caspar decreed to celebrate the journey of the three kings to Bethlehem every year and to call the celebration Christmas. At the end of the festivities, a gift is given by King Caspar and his family to each person to remember what took place in Bethlehem.

Chapter IX

Sharing Peace and Goodwill

Arabia, April, 1 AD

After the excitement of his homecoming celebration and retelling the story of their encounter with the thieves and King Herod, Ezra spends the next few days in quiet solitude. The understanding and willingness of his parents to help him is unexpected after telling the truth about Hannah. Weighing each possible scenario carefully and knowing how much Hannah is committed to helping her aunt and uncle, he realizes that even if the debt is repaid, she might not want to return with him. What if the fur trader's son disagreed with having the debt repaid in cash only and insisted that Hannah's hand in marriage must be included to repay the debt? *What then?* He asks himself. However, he believes that if Hannah feels the same for him as he does for her, then their only chance for happiness will be lost if he doesn't go north. He starts planning for the long journey.

Ezra informs his mother and father of his decision. With helpful advice from his father's best guide, together they plan for the shortest route and for the supplies needed. The guide is also skilled in speaking other languages. Four guards, two guides, and two servants will make the journey with Prince Ezra. They prepare for light provisions, so traveling would be faster, and all will be on horseback followed by two horse-drawn carts.

Knowing the journey will be long and rough, Ezra selects the best of his young and strong unwedded guards from many who volunteered. They also select the best horses with the most stamina and speed. They wear disguises—dressed as ordinary traders who are traveling constantly, looking for trading opportunities. The guards keep their weapons out of sight, not wanting to attract any attention to the gold pieces for Hannah's uncle. Guards with weapons make it obvious that they are protecting valuables or members of a royal family. As an extra precaution, the bottoms of four water jugs are the hiding place for the gold coins. Ezra and his men are ready, and all anticipate an exciting journey. Caspar is satisfied with their preparation and allows them to leave just as their cold season ended.

Progress every day is better than they have anticipated. Their disguise as common traders work as planned, and they remain alone except for giving directions to other travelers. Not using the same route used by Ezra previously, they are careful to follow the planned course. The faster route will improve their chances of being in Tobolsk sooner. Looking to the heavens for guidance, Ezra once again finds the star that leads him north. He has confidence in their planned route and is hopeful that he will reach Hannah in time before she marries Ivan.

As they travel, Ezra shares his many different experiences with the men. Occasionally they pass through a village or town he remembers. He stops to visit friends who offered shelter and food on his first journey, and offers a gift in appreciation for their help and to commemorate his journey to Bethlehem. He shares the story of Bethlehem and about the star that led three wise kings from faraway places to offer Jesus gifts. He tells of the angel who appeared before the shepherds who gave them the message of the blessed event. All who heard of Jesus marked the day of his birth, a day the Christ Child was born, and a day they would celebrate peace, a celebration of giving, decreed by his father to be Christmas.

Tobolsk, Siberia August, 1 AD

Four months pass since starting the journey north. The long summer days are shorter, and Ezra recognizes the landscape of the northland. The familiar fragrance of tall pine trees and spruce that skirt the steep mountains awakens memories of meeting Hannah in Herald's cave. The air is cooler, and atop the peaks of mountains, snow clings to jagged rocks. Making their way through a narrow mountain pass, Ezra recalls the tragic loss of Hannah's parents and his own brush with death. It is here in this pass that the mountain fell on him. While passing through, all eyes look upward. No one speaks as if they expect danger at any moment.

Ezra is beginning to feel anxious and excited as he anticipates meeting Hannah. Soon the town of Tobolsk where she lives comes into view. Ezra informs his men that they would reach Tobolsk by the end of the day.

The dark shadows of the trees give way to the sunlight, and the sun warms their cold moist skin on their faces. The scent of the trees gradually ushers in the fragrance of grassland and streams. The town is near, and Ezra will soon find out if Hannah has gotten married. His excitement turns into uneasiness. He takes a deep breath and fights the urge to hurry the pace. Ezra's men all know of the circumstances between Hannah and her uncle, and they encourage Ezra to go ahead. However, Ezra remembers what he has planned and why. It will not be wise to show too much enthusiasm in case Hannah is already married.

At the outskirts of Tobolsk, the stable belonging to Igor comes into view. He can hear the sound of a blacksmith's hammer forming metal. The scent of smoke from a kiln mixed with the pungent odor of dung from the stable fills the air. Ezra reaches for the medal hanging from his neck. The truth of their love is near. He squeezes the medal through his shirt, takes a deep breath hoping for the best, and approaches Hannah's uncle Igor who is just leading a horse out.

"Greetings, Igor," Ezra calls out. "It is nice to see you once again. Do you have room in your stables to rest and care for our horses?"

Igor stops in his tracks, staring at Ezra and his men, unsure of who they are, and then returning the greeting. "Greetings to you also, yes, I can tend to your horses. But I'm afraid while you look familiar, I don't recall your name as you do mine. I apologize."

"No apologies needed, Igor," Ezra replies as he and the others dismount their horses. "I'm Ezra. I was lost in the hillside a long time ago before your last winter. You, your wife Ira, and niece Hannah helped me prepare for my journey home."

"Oh yes, Ezra! I remember you now. It's nice to see you again. You are not lost again, are you?" Igor asks approaching Ezra.

"Oh no, Igor, we're not lost. I told my father the story Herald told me of the star falling from the sky where the lake is now. In our kingdom, my father King Casper is known as a wise man who studies the stars. I've been sent here to find pieces of the star so he can study it and record his observations," Ezra answers, sounding like he is on an official expedition.

"Who did you say talked about the star falling?" Igor asks.

"Herald, the one who lives in the cave near the lake, Hannah's brother."

"Hannah's brother?" Igor asks. "Hannah has no brother, much less one who lives in a cave." Igor chuckles "That crazy one who calls himself Herald and tells stories? I warned Hannah not to spend too much time with him. I know he is kind and will not hurt children, but some children believe in his stories and are disappointed and hurt when they find the stories are not true. Herald told Hannah that a prince would take her away from here one day and convinced her that you were the prince. She hoped that you would take her away. I convinced her otherwise, the custom of royal families is that a prince marries only a princess. As for you being a prince, a prince would not have traveled alone and got lost as you did. Isn't that right, Ezra? Yes, it's a good thing she went off with Ivan. Or she would have become old waiting for her prince."

Not prepared for receiving that information immediately, Ezra tries to remain calm. "Well, yes! It is good for Hannah that Ivan took her for a wife. I hope she finds happiness, Igor."

"Oh no, Ezra, you are mistaken," Igor explains. "Ivan will not take her for a wife yet. It is our custom that the groom's family receives a dowry in order to marry. I have tried and will continue to try to save enough money, but business is not good enough yet to save for her dowry. Ivan was gracious to accept her now as his servant until I pay the dowry. Then he will marry her. For now, I hope I saved her the hardship of having to live with us. She is at the age of marriage now, and she should start her own life, shouldn't she, Ezra?"

Ezra thinks for a while, unsure of what he can say. "Yes, Igor, she is a young beautiful maiden now, and ready for marriage." Ezra needs time to think this through. For the moment, he directs his men to unpack, unsaddle the horses, and take them into the stable.

Ezra's plan of giving Igor a gift will make matters worse. If Igor has enough money for Hannah's dowry, Ivan will take Hannah for his wife. It is a simple decision to change his mind and not give the gift to Igor, thereby preventing the marriage. However, it would mean that his original intention of giving a gift without receiving something in return is under false pretenses. Ezra knows in his heart what he must do.

Ezra calls out to Igor, who is showing his men where to put the horses. "Igor, do you and your wife Ira have time tonight after supper to meet with me?"

"Tonight, well, yes, I think we can. What do you have in mind, Ezra?" Igor questions, curious to know why Ezra feels he has to ask, sounding very official. Ezra should have known that Ira and he would be delighted to have him visit.

Ezra offers a short explanation to satisfy Igor's curiosity. "After we unpack and before we rest for the night, I would like to give you a gift and share a story with you about a blessed event that took place in Bethlehem after I returned home. All who have heard the story as I traveled acknowledged the blessed event and will celebrate it as a special day each year as Christmas."

Igor accepts the reason. "Ezra, it seems very important that you share this with all you meet on your journey. Yes, Ira and I would like to hear of this event, but why the gift, Ezra?"

"I will explain tonight, Igor."

The prince and his men finish the task of unpacking and prepare a campsite near the stable. After supper, Ezra removes the gold pieces from the bottom of the water jugs and prepares to visit Igor and Ira. He asks two of the guards and one servant to accompany him, dressed in their best palace attire, and he will be dressed as Prince Ezra, son of King Caspar. They take hot baths, shave off their beards, and apply lotions to freshen their skin, while special care is taken in dressing to be sure that they look their best. The guards talk to each other of how good it feels to wear their armor and bear their swords and lances. They are proud to be part of the select few who are chosen to protect and serve their prince. The servant picks up the small bags of gold pieces. With Prince Ezra leading, they leave the campsite to walk the short distance to Igor's the birthday of Jesus.

Igor expects Ezra's arrival and looks out the window upon hearing the sound of approaching footsteps on the gravel path. Surprised by the approaching group of men dressed as he has never seen, he calls out to Ira. He isn't sure who they are.

As Igor reaches to open the door, Ira asks, "Who are these men?"

"I'm not sure," Igor answers, looking bewildered. "They come as if they are expected," he says as he opens the door. "Good evening, how may I help you tonight?" greets Igor.

"Good evening, Igor, good evening, Ira, we are here as we arranged, to honor you with a gift and to tell you of a blessed event," announces Ezra.

Igor is speechless and looks even more bewildered.

Ezra expects Igor will not recognize them and continue his greeting. "Maybe you've forgotten, Igor, and don't expect us. If we have come at a bad time, we can return later. Igor, I'm Prince Ezra, son of King Caspar of Arabia, and these are my palace guards and servant. I hope we haven't alarmed you and Ira. We didn't mean to. My humble apologies if we did."

Igor remains speechless, still unsure of whom they are, and repeat what they say. "Did you say you are Prince Ezra, son of King Caspar?"

"Yes, I did, Igor. I am Prince Ezra, the same prince who had worked in your stable last year and trained the young stallion I named Shamal, remember?"

With that, Ira kicks Igor on the back of his heel while trying to remain composed, but is obviously embarrassed. She whispers loudly in Igor's ear. "Why didn't you tell me Ezra is a real prince? Neither I nor you are prepared to properly entertain such a guest in our home."

Then in a more cordial tone and smiling at Ezra, she says, "I'm sorry, your highness, please forgive the stupidity of Igor. I fear he has been kicked on the head too often by the horses he will be sleeping with tonight. Please come in."

Ira bows in reverence and steps aside, showing the way with a gentle gesture of her hand. As Ezra and his men walk past them, she kicks Igor once more as she walks by, all the while smiling and admiring Prince Ezra.

Prince Ezra offers an explanation. "Ira, don't be so upset at Igor. He would not have known. We were dressed as common traders who roam the lands in search of trade. We chose to dress that way because of what I need to tell you, and as strange as it may sound, I hope you believe what I say to be the truth. But first, I wish you would join me in some tea. If you will allow my servant Nicholas to use your kitchen, he will prepare the finest tea from our kingdom."

Igor answers, unsure of how and what to say, "Yes, Ezra, I'm sorry, your highness, prince. We would be honored to join you. Ira, would you please help in the kitchen."

Ezra stops her. "No, Ira, I'm sure my servant will not need your assistance. Pretend you are my guest, and experience the pleasure of being waited on by Nicholas, the best servant in our palace. I have much to tell you, and I fear it may be too late."

"Oh no, Prince Ezra, there is lots of time, the hour is not late," says Igor.

"I don't mean late that way, Igor, I mean too late for Hannah and I."

"Hannah and you?" repeats Ira with great interest and surprise.

"Yes, Ira. I've returned here to ask Hannah to return with me as a guest to our kingdom. My father King Caspar and mother Queen Malana both extended a personal invitation for her to be our guest if she would like. I have a written invitation here with my father's seal. It is written in your language. If you wonder how it is we know your language, my father is a very wise man who not only studies the stars but also many other languages and cultures. My guide is also skilled in many languages, and both have taught me to speak it."

"But I've told you Hannah no longer lives with us, Prince Ezra," says Igor. "She left with Ivan ten days ago to bargain for and collect fur from trappers. I fear I've made I terrible mistake by allowing Ivan to take her, Prince Ezra, your highness. In fact, I see now, I've made several terrible mistakes. I did not believe you or her that you were a prince. Why didn't you ask her to return with you then, Prince Ezra?"

"I did not for three reasons, I was sure then that my father would not permit me to be in a relationship with someone not of the same culture or customs as we are. Since then, I learned different. The other is Hannah said her hand had been promised in marriage to Ivan by you Igor, in payment to Ivan's father for the stable business."

Igor admits, feeling heavy in heart. "Yes, Prince Ezra, I'm afraid I did such a thing, and I'm afraid Hannah understands too much of how difficult it is for me to make enough to pay what I owe. Please believe me when I tell you.

Hannah misunderstands the arrangement of paying the fur trader. Yes, I do owe him money, but only if Hannah did not agree to be Ivan's servant, but now I only need to pay a dowry, just any small amount of gold, to keep true to our traditions, and they can be properly married," Igor goes on to explain.

"When I got married to Ira, we wanted our own business. I didn't have enough to buy the stable outright. I worked for Adolph in this stable. As a wedding gift, he offered to sell us the stable at a very low price, and I was to pay for it from money I earned from the business. For many years after, I tried very hard to pay Adolph what I owed. But in the contract, I agreed not to charge the fur trader the full amount for my services, because I thought he was being very generous. I know now it was foolish for me to agree.

"Since, I haven't been able to save enough money for the payment, Adolph asked to take Hannah for his son Ivan as payment, but he would not agree to marriage. As I said earlier, it is customary that the father of the bride gives a dowry if he wished her daughter to be married."

"Can Hannah break the engagement?"

"No, Prince Ezra, your highness, I don't think so. My only hope now is to earn what little gold I need for her dowry so she can be properly married. I fear I've made a foolish decision when I agreed to Adolph's terms. Perhaps Ira is right; I've been kicked in my head too often by my horses that are as stubborn as I am."

"Igor, don't feel heavy-hearted over decisions you made. I believe you acted only in the best interest of your family. It seems Adolph has taken advantage of your fine blacksmith's skills and generous heart. Igor, you don't realize how you have lifted a heavy burden from my heart and how I may also lift your burden. First, I must continue with what I'm telling you so the truth as to why I made this return journey is known to you and Ira.

"Last of all, but the most important reason why I did not ask Hannah to leave with me is that Herald asked me to deliver his gift to Bethlehem for the infant Christ child who will be king of the Jews. I had a compelling feeling that I was destined by God to go on the journey to Bethlehem and present the gift. This brings me to the subject for which I asked to come tonight and must tell you."

Ezra tells the story of his journey to Bethlehem and meeting with the other two kings. How the angels appeared from the heavens to the shepherds and Joseph. He tells also of how Herald knew he was a prince and of his coming to the north. He tells of the strange powers of the box that Herald had given as a gift. Most importantly, he tells of the birth of Jesus and how his birth symbolizes a gift of peace for all people of the great continents and all those who have heard of Jesus will make it special by celebrating his birth.

Igor and Ira are taken by what Prince Ezra shared with them, about how destiny guided seemingly random events and people toward the birth of Jesus. For a few moments, they are silent. They believe, but are also mystified over the chain of miracles leading to this moment. If they believe in Hannah and Herald, Hannah would not be forced to be a servant for Ivan. Ira begins to weep.

Through her sobbing and tears, she looks at Igor for consolation. "Oh my, Igor, what have we done to our dear Hannah? Why did we not trust her heart? As Prince Ezra said, now it might be too late. I fear by now Ivan has taken her as his mistress. She will give in to him, because she would feel it is her duty. She is all alone with no one to talk to and no one to comfort her." Ira continues to cry out and walks over to the doorway of Hannah's empty room. Ira grieves even more, her anguish too much to bear, flooding her eyes with tears. She falls on Hannah's bed as if to absorb her spirit, her scent, and begs for Hannah's forgiveness. Igor too is taken over by his anguish and goes to Ira's side and weeps for Hannah, as only a father can weep for his daughter.

Ezra looks in the direction of his servant who has entered the room with tea. Ezra thanks him and asks him to pour two cups for Ira and Igor and to take it to them on a tray with the three bags of gold pieces. Ezra follows his servant to Hannah's room where Ira and Igor are sitting on the edge of her bed, side by side, head-to-head, in each other's arms, not weeping anymore, but simply staring at the floor.

Ezra calls out softly. "Ira, Igor, please, listen to what I say. It's from the very depth of my soul that I say this. I would be honored if you allow me to help lift your burden. I don't mean to insult you by offering this gift in hopes that it would relieve the anguish you are feeling. I too feel the same loss as you do, and maybe by some miracle of this gift, our burden along with Hannah's can be taken from us. Throughout my recent experience, I've learned that I must trust those I say I love. They, in return, will trust in my love for them. I believe deep in my heart; Hannah and I know of that trust. Although we did not speak of it through our lips, we spoke of it through our hearts. I know Hannah will do everything in her power to wait for my return. That is why you must let me help release the grip of Adolph from you and Hannah. If you agree, I will find her.

"I offer this gift of gold pieces to you, Igor and Ira, and expect nothing in return. You may do with it whatever you wish. I offer it because you are very generous to many who travel and are in need of help, not only me, and you ask nothing in return.

"Igor, Ira, please, know that what I say is from my heart. If you wish to pay your debt and also the dowry so Hannah is happy and may properly marry

Ivan, then so be it. I will not try to convince you or her otherwise. I will simply collect rocks from the star that makes a special metal and return home."

The servant kneels on one knee in front of Igor and Ira and offers the tea and the bags of gold pieces. They thank the servant for the tea but are hesitant in taking the bags of gold. Igor pauses for a moment thinking of what to say.

Igor breaks his silence. "Prince Ezra, your Highness, you are noble indeed. We believe you are sincere, but we cannot accept your gift." Igor looks at Ira and continues. "We know you are hopeful of having Hannah return with you, and we also believe Hannah would like to go with you. We would be happy for you both if indeed you marry. In accepting your generous gift now, it would only serve to have me feel indebted to you, and I fear Hannah would feel the same also. It would taint the purity of the love you two would have for each other. I should have never bought this business in the first place. Ira, Hannah, and I would have all been happier today. She would have been free to follow her heart, and her dream of marrying a prince would have come true. Instead, it is a very sad day."

Igor and Ira remain silent, staring at the floor. For them, it seems the burden of guilt can never be taken away. Prince Ezra has no other option now but to collect the rocks for his father and return home.

"Prince Ezra, if I may offer a suggestion?" says his servant as he rises from his kneeling position.

"Of course, you may, Nicholas," Ezra answers.

Humbly, the servant offers his solution. "With all due respect, Prince Ezra, in times of great emotional stress, often a simple solution to a problem is overlooked. Igor, are you willing to sell the business if you could for an amount enough to pay your debt, thereby freeing you from the fur trader's control and also pay a dowry to whoever Hannah would want to marry?"

"Yes, I would. No one in this town would purchase it at a fair price, especially with the influence of Adolph," Igor replies.

The servant continues, "Prince Ezra, isn't it in the best interest of the monarchy that a trade center owned by the kingdom is established in a northern frontier, where the finest furs are collected and traded?"

"Yes, my trusted Nicholas," the prince answers, excited as he realizes immediately what his servant is suggesting. "It would be a very wise investment for our kingdom. We would also need a trustworthy master blacksmith, who could run the affairs of the trade center and stable, and I know of no one better than you Igor that our kingdom could trust. Ira, we would need you as well." Prince Ezra, Igor, and Ira are eager over the idea.

"You would need me, Prince Ezra? Ira asks, smiling and surprised that she is needed in this promising idea.

"Yes Ira," the prince replies. "I believe it is you who made Hannah's fine fur coat I saw last winter?"

"Yes, Prince Ezra, it was I," Ira answers.

"Very well then," Prince Ezra explains. "You will select the finest fur from trappers and make coats worthy for kings and queens. You will offer the best prices and supplies to the trappers. It will be difficult for Adolph to use his influence and control the trade of furs and supplies. So now I ask you officially, in the name of my father, King Caspar. Will you sell this stable business to our kingdom and also be willing to work and make the trade center profitable and share the profits equally?"

Igor and Ira look at one another for a moment, and each nod their heads and smile, and then embrace each other. They thank Prince Ezra and his servant Nicholas. While enjoying tea with Prince Ezra, they give directions to the remote campsite where the trappers and Adolph traded.

CHAPTER X

A Struggle between Peace and Conflict

he next morning, Prince Ezra and his men are up early, preparing to leave in search for Hannah. They inform Igor that they will go to the cave and ask Herald where and when he last saw Hannah. Within minutes, they are at the entrance of the cave. Prince Ezra is somewhat cautious when entering, because the bear named Boris could be in the cave. He calls out softly at first to Herald through the barrier, before pushing it aside. He calls louder as he makes his way past the barrier and waits for his eyes to adjust to the dark, and still, no reply. He moves into the darkness and finds the cave without any candles burning. He calls out to his guards to come in and to bring torches for light.

Ezra and his guards find no one in the cave. The tables, chairs, and bedding in the main room and Hannah's room are where he last remembers. He asks his guide Nubar, also an excellent tracker, to look for signs of anyone leaving the cave recently. Nubar discovers tracks about two days old and identifies one of the footprints belonging to a man, but there are other strange animal footprints following the man. Prince Ezra determines those to be of Boris and the reindeer, and the man, probably Herald. He instructs the two servants, one guide and one guard, to remain at the cave until they return, and if Herald returns, to tell him that he, Prince Ezra, is back and is looking for Hannah.

Prince Ezra heads out into the tundra beyond the hills surrounding Star Lake. The land is mostly barren with trees spaced far apart and outcrops of tall bushes, large rocks, some as large as a palace, scattered in between short patches of grass. The hills gently roll up and down as sand in the desert. The landscape is laced with small streams and ponds. Occasionally, they see a fox running to find refuge in a hole or a mink scampering to the nearest pond or stream to hide from them. The small animals, as told by Ira, are the animals that provided the finest furs. The air smells of berries, a favored delicacy of the bears in the tundra. They are warned by Igor to stay away from them, for they can be as swift as horses and as cunning as a hunter stalking prey.

Nubar also notices signs of older horses' hoof prints left by trappers perhaps a week ago. The trail follows Igor's directions to the fur trader's camp, and Prince Ezra is confident that they're on the right trail. They pick up the pace and ride at a slow canter, resting occasionally while checking the tracks and their direction. With just a few hours' rest tonight, they could reach the campsite by late afternoon the next day. The daylight hours are much shorter this far north, but the moon will be bright enough to cast shadows and provide adequate light to travel by night.

As the sun slowly touches the distant horizon, Ezra and his men reach a small hilltop from where they see the vastness of the tundra completely surrounding them. Just beyond eyesight on the far north horizon, a steep, white-capped mountain as Igor has described rises from the plains of the tundra. Adolph's campsite is located at the base of that mountain.

Ezra's eyes follow the trail winding its way toward the distant mountains. In the shadows of the lower hills and valleys, not far from where they are, Ezra notices a small cluster of trees next to a pile of large rocks beside the trail. Ezra points at it. "See that large bank of rocks next to trail? It's about an hour to walk our horses. Let's slow our pace and cool the horses, then rest for a few hours there."

Suddenly, they hear a loud roar in the distance. The crickets stop chirping and the flocks of birds take off in flight startled by the sound that breaks the silence of the tundra. They look at each other to be sure all hear it. The roar is unmistakable as they hear it again.

"What is it?" one of the guards asks.

"I'm not sure," says Ezra. "But only one beast in this land can command a powerful roar as that. I believe it's a bear."

They hear the roar again and talk quietly among themselves, trying to determine where it's coming from. They wait for another. A few minutes pass, and still no roar. They continue to walk their horses slowly down the trail, looking carefully in the heavy brush. Nubar leads the way ahead of the prince, and the guards take up positions surrounding the prince, one on each side, and one behind. They grip their lances and swords to be ready in case anything threatens the safety of the prince.

The day gives way to dark, and the moon is already high in the heavens. Stars shine like jewels between the clouds. And suddenly, as if an angel in heaven is shooting a flaming arrow through the sky above them, a streak of light passes directly over their heads.

Ezra remarks, "That star seemed closer to the ground than what I've seen in the desert skies."

"Perhaps it's because we're so far north, we're closer to the heavens," Nubar explains.

"Perhaps," they all agree and continue forward.

Approaching the cluster of trees and large rocks, the horses begin to get skittish. They hesitate in their steps as the riders urge them forward with kicks to their sides. The closer the horses get to the trees, the more they fight not to go forward and rear up on their hind legs, snorting and whinnying in protest.

Ezra tries to control the tone of his voice and is careful not to startle the horses even more. As he struggles to stay in control of his horse, short breaths interrupt his voice while giving orders to his men. "Turn around. Stay calm. Walk the horses back up the trail, dismount, and calm them down," he says trying to be calm.

Once the horses are settled, the men sigh in relief. "Keep a watchful eye in those trees and rocks, something in there frightens the horses," one of the guards warns.

"What do you want us to do, Prince Ezra?" another guard asks, acknowledging that he is ready to defend the prince.

"The horses are calm here, so there appears to be no immediate danger. Let's rest here but keep a watchful eye for any signs of movement. It could have been the bear we heard roaring that scared the horses," Ezra suggests.

They wait quietly, straining to see through the darkness of the night. Ezra breaks the silence. "Three of us should go forward on foot and look for what caused the horses to bolt. Sooner or later, we will need to pass."

"So be it," the guards answer as they ready their crossbows.

They quickly discuss how they will move forward ready for any threat. Nubar will be a few steps forward with a lance and will hold a small lantern on the point to see what may be ahead. One guard would be on each side of the guide, a few steps back with crossbows drawn. Ezra will be in the center with a long lance. The third guard will stay with the horses and watch the rear with another crossbow drawn.

They move forward slowly and reach the area where the horses start to become skittish. They pause for a moment, looking carefully in the dark shadows of the trees and rocks. Nothing is moving. Crickets are chirping as they would on a calm quiet night. They are now closer than before with the horses. Ahead, Nubar moves the lance to position the lantern closer to something on the ground next to a tree. He signals them to stop and be quiet.

He moves toward a dark shadow on the ground, then stops suddenly and jerks back, frozen in his footsteps. The others wait for a sign. Nubar is motionless as the lantern swings back and forth on the tip of his lance, and all others remain motionless, also not knowing what Nubar has seen.

Finally, Nubar signals to move up slowly. The guards aim their crossbows at the large, dark shadow on the ground as they cautiously join Nubar with Ezra behind them.

They are close enough now to see what has frightened the horses. They see blood on the ground next to the large beast Ezra recognizes as a bear lying motionless. A large metal jaw with sharp teeth is clamped on one of the bear's front paws, but the injury doesn't look to be serious enough to have killed the bear. It appears to be breathing.

"Is it sleeping?" Nubar asks.

"I don't know," Ezra replies. "The metal jaw is chained to the tree, so if it awakens, we should be safe. Throw a rock on it and see if it will come to," he suggests.

Nubar throws a small rock, but the bear doesn't move. "It must be unconscious. Maybe the metal jaw is poisonous like a snake and made the bear sleep," says Nubar, then throws another rock. "From the size of his paws, this is the bear we followed, the one you call Boris."

"If it is, then where are Herald and the reindeer?" Ezra asks. The prince calls out to Herald, and Nubar checks for footprints left by Herald. No one answers, puzzling Ezra. "I don't understand, why did he leave Boris? I wonder if Herald has gone ahead to the trappers' campsite to get help" Ezra asks himself.

"Prince Ezra!" Nubar shouts.

Ezra joins Nubar in a flat grassy area off the trail. "What is it?" he asks.

"Prince Ezra, I don't understand," Nubar explains. "I checked the trail ahead, and there are no fresh hoof prints leading away from this rest stop but these. Look at how the hoof prints simply stop, and there is none that turns around." Then Nubar shows Ezra how Herald's footprints are between hoof prints of two reindeer walking then disappears. To add to the confusion, the reindeer hoof prints run a few steps more then also disappears.

"I don't have any explanation for you. I'm afraid I'm more confused than you," says Ezra. "Let's rest a while longer and bring the horses here to show them Boris is harmless. They will not be afraid if they see us with Boris."

"It will be done," agrees Nubar.

Nubar gathers wood to make a small fire while the guards tend to the horses.

Boris lies motionless while Ezra examines him carefully. He checks the wound and finds it still bleeding from where the metal jaw has bitten through the thick skin. Ezra tries pulling the jaw apart, and it opens slightly. He knows that two strong guards and their lances can pry it open and free Boris. The problem then would be what Boris might do to them if he gains consciousness. Ezra knows, however, that leaving Boris trapped is not an option. They must try to free Boris. Herald has a reason for taking Boris to where Hannah lives with the trappers and fur traders. He can only guess that Herald knows Hannah is in danger and needs Boris to protect her.

He discusses the options with his men. They agree that the sooner they remove the metal jaw and medicine is applied, the better chances are for healing. They decide to tie Boris to the tree using all the ropes they have. A quick getaway is planned with the horses by moving them past Boris, the trees, and large rocks. If Boris awakes and struggles free, they will simply ride off toward the traders' campsite.

The two strongest guards try to pry the jaws open. They open it slightly, but then it stops. The jaw is held closed by something other than the springs that clamp it shut. They examine it closer. Not seeing anything like this before, they marvel at how ingenious it is. The guards keep trying to open it, but it only makes the wound worse.

Prince Ezra knows that soon they must leave and examines the metal jaw once again. He needs to find a way to remove it. While examining the jaw, a familiar voice calls out to him.

"Prince Ezra, your highness, do you need my help?" a familiar voice asks.

Ezra turns around along with his men and sees a man approaching the fire. As the man gets closer, the fire reveals who he is.

"Igor?" they all shout together.

"Igor, what are you doing here?" Ezra asks more confused than surprised.

"Herald brought me here to help Boris," replies Igor.

"Brought you here? How could he? And where is he?" Ezra wonders out loud, even more confused now. "What happened to Boris only happened an hour ago. We have traveled all day to reach here. I don't understand. I thought we followed Herald. How was he able to go by us without being seen and return in such a short time with you?" Ezra asks, seeing but still not believing Igor.

"Greetings, Prince Ezra," another familiar voice beyond the light of the fire is heard.

"Is that you, Herald?" Ezra asks still hearing, seeing but not believing.

"Yes, it is I," Herald says quietly. "I knew you would return, and just in time to rescue Hannah. Igor has told me everything you did for them and also about the gift I gave you from the cave dwellers and how you offered it to the newborn child Jesus."

Ezra is confused and questions Herald. "But, Herald, we followed your footprints all day and did not see you pass us!"

"Yes, yes, yes, I know all that. I used a secret trail that's a shortcut. Now let's take care of Boris so we can rescue Hannah. I will tell you of the shorter trail later, Prince Ezra, after Igor removes the steel trap. Hurry, Igor! Boris will awake soon, and I must cleanse his wounds with water from Star Lake," orders Herald.

"Yes, Herald, I have seen this trap before. This belongs to Adolph. He intended to use it to trap bears for the first time this season. It is something new he designed, and I made it for him. It's easy to remove, just remove this pin, and the clamp will release its grip." With that said, Igor pulls on the pin and the steel trap is loose enough to remove from Boris's paw.

Herald orders everyone to stand back, asking them not to show Boris the crossbows or lances when he awakes. Everyone quickly obliges and waits beyond the light of the fire. Herald pours water from his sack onto Boris's bloody paw and rinses the dry blood and mud from the wound. Herald is the only one close to Boris, and all watch as he bows his head in reverence after looking to the heavens. The others look at each other, and then they also bow their heads when Prince Ezra bows. Herald ends his prayer and pours water into the mouth of Boris, then he rises to his feet and joins the others.

"Boris will be awake soon, and he will be able to walk. Please remove the ropes from him now and continue on your way to the campsite. Hurry! Hannah may be in danger," Herald pleads.

"Why do you say she is in danger, Herald?" Ezra asks, trying not to let his panic show.

"Because of this," Herald tries to control his anger as he pulls a piece of Hannah's clothing from his bag. "Adolph tore this off Hannah and used it to bait the trap to catch Boris. I found it here by the trap after Boris got caught. It could only mean they intend to harm her. They know that Boris would follow her and protect her. So hurry! Go now, Prince Ezra! Boris, Igor, and I will catch up with you later," Herald demands, still trying to control his anger.

Ezra and his men mount their horses and start on an easy canter away from the rest stop.

At the fur traders' campsite, trappers are sitting around the fire laughing. One of the trappers shout out, "Hey, Ivan! You think you'll be lucky tonight?" The others laugh. Another yells, "Hey, Ivan! Do you need help from us?" The roar of laughter is louder, then they stop as they remain quiet, listening for any response.

From Hannah's tent, a loud slap is heard, and Hannah's stern voice can be heard throughout the campsite. "I told you, Ivan, I will not be your mistress or your wife, until I know my uncle's obligation to pay a dowry is cancelled by your father. My uncle has paid his debt many times over by not charging you and your trappers fairly for his services."

"But, Hannah, I still don't understand why you agreed to come here," Ivan grumbles in a loud whisper, trying not to be heard by the trappers. "You agreed to be my mistress until your uncle pays your dowry."

Hannah calms herself and speaks gently to Ivan. "Ivan, I have already told you why I came with you. I beg you, please listen to me. Don't be like your father who takes advantage of people. Ivan, you and I have grown up together like sister and brother, and many in our town believe we would be happy together and wish us happiness. But I believe your father only used that knowledge to take advantage of my uncle's craftsmanship as a master blacksmith without having to pay him fairly. I decided to come with you because I want you to ask your father to cancel my uncle's obligation to pay a dowry. Only then will there be any hope for you and I. I'm willing then to try to make you happy if you desire it. If I'm forced to, as I am now, I will only despise you and your father. I would rather die before I'll be your mistress."

"Hannah, yes, I do understand, and yes, I too feel like you are more my sister as I am your brother. But my father tells me that I'll become a man by the end of this trading season, because I will take you for a mistress." Ivan is distressed and feels sorry for Hannah. "I fear Hannah, it's been over ten days now, and my father is growing impatient. He has told me he will use you to trade for the best furs if you do not cooperate. Tell me, what can we do?"

"Ivan, will you help me?" pleads Hannah. Ivan nods his head.

"Oh, Ivan, I knew you have a good heart, now listen carefully," says Hannah, with spirits lifted, smiling, and is greatly relieved to know she will survive one more night without being attacked. Hannah wonders if Boris will show up tomorrow while the trappers are away. Also, tomorrow Adolph plans to take a trip farther north to another outpost to deliver supplies, and Ivan will be out with their men to check the traps.

Hannah tells Ivan of her plan to help him and also to get herself out of this mess. She tells him they will pretend he has taken her for his mistress, thereby proving his manhood, and maybe Ivan could convince his father to cancel Igor's obligation. Ivan agrees and prepares to carry out Hannah's plan.

Outside, the trappers are still joking about Ivan. "Ivan should have remained with his mother," one trapper comments. Then another says, "Tomorrow Adolph wants us to show him our traps, maybe he needs us to babysit instead while he takes supplies to the northern outpost. Listen, Ivan and Hannah are carrying on again," says a trapper.

"Woman, I have had enough of your nonsense," Ivan says out loud, so all can hear. "Now do as I say, or you'll not see the light of day."

"Oh, Ivan, please don't hurt me," Hannah cries out, sounding fearful. "You're much too strong for me to resist anymore. Please be gentle, Ivan."

Ivan blows out the candle in Hannah's tent.

The trappers look at each other and nod their heads in approval. One of them comments, "Maybe he is like Adolph after all. You know what they say, like father like son." They all laugh, and one asks, "Where is that old miser anyway?" and another answer. "Where else, in bed with his money," all laugh again and call it a night.

At the break of day, Prince Ezra and his men stop to rest. Men and horses are tired from riding all night. The saddles are taken off the horses, and a fire is made for tea. A few hours of rest is needed since none has been taken since they found Boris. Weary from the ride, all are quiet as each one prepares a comfortable spot to nap. Prince Ezra looks at the snowcapped mountains where the traders' campsite is located. The rugged cliffs and ridges are now visible.

He wonders if he will be able to reach Hannah in time. The vision of Hannah is etched in his mind as he last saw her when she gave him the medal. Will she still look at him as she did then when they meet again later this day? The wild flowers of the tundra remind him of the fragrance from her hair. He closes his eyes and imagines embracing her with her head close to his heart. He takes a deep breath to capture the essence of her spirit in the depth of his soul. He calls out her name softly toward the snowcapped mountains as he releases his breath.

Prince Ezra turns around to find his men sleeping. Even the guard standing watch has fallen asleep, sitting up against a rock. The horses are grazing nearby and lift their heads to look, turning their ears when Ezra walks back to add more wood to the fire. The tea is ready, and he pours himself a cup. He walks over to the guard on watch and slowly removes the lance still clutched in the guard's hand with his helmet tilted forward on his head about to fall off. He spoke softly to the guard. "Sleep well, my trusted friend, today I may need your protection if Adolph challenges our ownership of the stables and Hannah's right to leave if she chooses."

In the traders' campsite, noises of trappers preparing to leave the campsite awaken Hannah from a deep sleep. Since reaching a mutual understanding with Ivan, she is able to sleep without worry that Ivan will try to take advantage of her. Rubbing her eyes, she remembers Ivan has fallen asleep on the floor. She quickly looks for him but finds herself alone in her tent. She gets out of her cot and peeks outside of the tent to find Ivan with the trappers getting ready to leave. Remembering their plan to pretend a passionate courtship is now mutually enjoyed, she calls out to Ivan in a provocative and alluring tone. "Ivan dear, must you leave me without a good-bye kiss?"

Ivan answers as they have planned. "Woman, can't you see I'm busy? When I return, I expect the bedding to be washed and ready for tonight."

"Yes, my dear Ivan, I will do as you say, my love," Hannah answers, blowing a kiss in his direction and disappearing into the tent. As she turns, she notices Ivan's father Adolph on horseback, followed by a supply wagon on the far side of the camp. He obviously had witnessed the exchange between Ivan and her. She is pleased the opportunity presented itself. *It is a lucky coincidence,* she thinks. Maybe today will be her lucky day. Hopefully Boris will find her today, and no one will dare stop her from leaving. Before leaving, she will have Boris hold Adolph to the ground until he agrees to sign a document, releasing her uncle from his debt.

From outside her tent, she hears the trappers and Adolph talking about her. They break out in laughter joking about Ivan's conquest. Hannah peeks through the opening of the doorway in time to see Ivan receive congratulatory handshakes and pats on the back from his father and the trappers before they all departed.

She remembers Adolph will be gone all day to deliver supplies to the northern outpost. Hoping she will be free to leave, she prepares clothing and supplies for her escape. She locates a whistle that Herald had made for her to use in calling Boris. She drops it in her coat pocket.

Hannah goes about her camp chores. Two older trappers who watch the campsite are also walking about, sorting and drying skins. The scent of rotting flesh from drying skins taints the air and lures hungry bears for miles. Surrounding the campsite, a high wall made of logs keeps them out. Entry to the campsite is through a large swinging gate. It is heavy and rests on the ground, needing two men to lift it and swing it open. Hannah asks the old trappers to open the gate for her so she can get water to boil and use it to bathe. While out of sight, she also plans to blow on the whistle to call Boris if he is near but out of sight. She is not concerned about being heard. Herald said only bears and dogs will hear the sound of the whistle.

A half day's ride away from the campsite, Prince Ezra and his men are under way once more. All, including Prince Ezra, have rested and eaten. Before leaving the rest stop, they talk of how they must be on guard while at the campsite. They have learned in their journey that their horses are worth more than their lives. Traders who travel alone or in small numbers are often killed just for their pack animals and horses.

Much farther away, Herald and Igor are following Boris, who has made a remarkable recovery from his injuries. Although Boris is large, he moves at a swift pace. Fortunately, Herald and Igor are riding the reindeer.

Igor is persistent in asking Herald questions of the strange short trail they used, and why Herald made him wear a hood. What was used to put Boris to sleep then heal the wounds, and finally what woke Boris up? The questions fall on deaf ears as Herald's attention is focused on Boris. Boris stops and has his nose high in the air, moving his head from side to side. He stands on his hind legs looking in the direction of the distant snowcapped mountains. Igor and Herald stop and look also.

"Herald, why don't you answer my questions about the shorter trail and hood over my head? And why was it necessary for me not to see where the shorter trail is located? It felt like we climbed a high mountain, then back down just before reaching Boris. What did you put in my tea? It seems like I lost track of time during the ride, it was too short. I looked for the mountain this morning but could not find it," Igor persists, insisting Herald answers his questions.

"Igor, I will tell you later. Last night you agreed to come with me because you were worried about Hannah, so let's be more concerned about finding her than how we got here," replies Herald.

"Herald, I find you a very strange and mysterious man. I feel I should believe you, but you have said many strange things. Yes, I admit the truth of Ezra being a prince and the gift made by the cave dwellers for the child King Jesus, but why do you say Hannah is your sister?" Igor asks.

Herald looks to the heavens for relief and answers, "Igor, this will be the last question I answer until we find Hannah. I claim Hannah as a sister as I would claim you as a brother. All people of the world have one father." Herald points to the sky. "I honor my father by treating all whom I meet as my sister and brother." Herald places his hands together as if to pray and bows slightly and reverently.

"Igor, I know you find it strange and hard to believe, as you did when you first heard of the cave dwellers when you were a child. Today you've found out, you should have believed. Perhaps before this day is over, you will also believe in the Father who watches over us. So, Igor, my brother, let's hurry and catch up with Boris, he is running faster, maybe he hears Hannah's whistle." Herald directs the two reindeer to push on. "Onward Recnad, Onward Recnarp!"

Back at the trader's campsite, Hannah is in her tent, taking her bath. She feels strange while getting water at the nearby stream, like someone was watching her from behind a cluster of trees and rocks at the base of the mountain. She looks back through the sparse growth of trees before walking through the gate but doesn't see anyone, and yet, she is sure. After drying herself and dressing, she pulls the curtain that partitioned her tent inside. She is startled to see Adolph sitting on her cot. "Adolph! … What is the meaning of this?" demands Hanna wanting an explanation, but she remembers quickly that Adolph is more easily persuaded by charm than harsh words. "I thought you traveled north to your outpost? To what do I owe this visit, Adolph? Hannah fakes a charming smile to hopefully convince Adolph that she is sincere in her relationship with Ivan.

"Well, Hannah," Adolph pauses, admiring Hannah's beauty. "So, you and Ivan are happy, are you?" he asks.

"Why, yes, Adolph. Can't you see that?" she answers. "Ivan and I have waited years for this time. Of course, we're happy."

"Then you won't mind if you never see your bear again, will you?" Adolph asks. "After all, it would be difficult to have a family with your bear by your side, wouldn't it?"

"Well, yes, Adolph," she agrees but is concerned. "But why do you bother yourself with the bear, Adolph?"

"Because you call for him and expect his arrival," he explains.

"Then it was you who was watching me at the stream, wasn't it?" Hannah asks, slightly disturbed but restrained.

"Well, yes, my horse had thrown a shoe, and as I returned, I saw you at the stream blowing your whistle," replies Adolph, sounding innocent of having an ulterior motive.

"Yes, you did see me blow the whistle. I did so just in case Boris did follow me. I do miss him. I'm afraid to be out there by myself without his protection," Hannah answers. "But is that all you have come here to discuss?"

"Why no, of course not, Hannah," he answers. "Ivan tells me if I cancel your uncle's obligation to pay a dowry, you would be very grateful. I came to find out just how grateful you would be."

"I would be very grateful, Adolph, I promise to be a good wife if he wants to marry, but yes, I would be very grateful," Hannah offers. "Would you cancel my uncle's obligation?" she asks again to be sure.

"I would, Hannah, but while Ivan enjoys your attention, it is I whom your uncle owes money to, not Ivan. It is I who wants your attention, not Ivan. Do you think for even one moment that I believe the charade you and Ivan carried out for my benefit? Don't you think I know my son better than you? Do you think you can fool me? I know he likes you as a sister only. He has begged me not to force you to marry him.

"Hannah, I have been without a wife for so many years I can't count. You've grown to be a very beautiful young woman. I am rich and can be a very generous man, but I have lost my patience. I will give you a choice, however, you can choose to be my mistress and have anything you want, or you can be a prostitute for whom the trappers will pay handsomely. And don't think that your uncle will ever make enough to pay his obligation for a dowry so you can marry. Anyway, who would want you for a wife then?" Adolph laughs.

Adolph continues to torment Hannah. "Oh, I forgot to tell you, if you wait for your bear, don't be surprised if he arrives with just three legs. My trappers who arrived late last night said that they heard an unmistakable roar of a bear caught in a trap we left at the last rest stop. I fear it is your bear, because I baited it with a piece of your clothing." Adolph laughs again, more cynical and eviler than humorous.

Hannah is devastated and loses her composure and screams at Adolph. "You are evil and disgusting, you filthy swine, get out! You are not concerned about Ivan's manhood, but you are more concerned about preserving yours. I will leave this place and never be your mistress or prostitute. I know my uncle Igor would have never allowed me to come had he known your evil intentions. When he finds out, he will seek you out and—"

Hannah is interrupted by Adolph. "And what Hannah, what can he do to me? If he could, he would have done it by now, don't you think?" Adolph departs, laughing arrogantly and telling her that she has until tonight on his return to decide.

Hannah's hopes are crushed. She falls on her cot sobbing, believing Igor, Ivan, and Boris are powerless to help her now. Now more than ever before, she has to escape. If she can get back to Tobolsk and tell her uncle about Adolph, he will believe her. Even though he is powerless to do anything to Adolph, he and Ira will at least stop Adolph from using her even if Igor has to give up the stable.

She hopes Ivan will help her escape. She knows Ivan often despises the way his father misuses his influence and power. Maybe the choices given to her by his father will be cause enough for Ivan to help her. She wonders if she should leave now or wait for Ivan. If she leaves now, there is enough daylight to be far away before Adolph returns. But traveling alone is dangerous. If she waits for Ivan, she might have to remain at the campsite overnight, and Ivan might not be able to help her without his father knowing or stop his father from using her.

She decides to leave a note explaining why she has to leave the campsite and asks him to meet her at the rest stop tonight and return with her to Tobolsk. If he does not arrive by midnight, she will understand and will continue without him. In her note, she explains she will tell the two old trappers that she has left for a long ride with Shamal toward the first rest stop and ask them to tell Ivan to join her so they can enjoy some time alone together under the moonlight.

Hannah's mind is set. She no longer feels sorry for herself, but is now more determined to leave and be free from Adolph's control. Better to try than to give up and die tormented, she tells herself.

Hannah quickly writes the note and places it on her bed. She hopes Ivan will come looking for her first before his father returns and finds her note. He should be able to leave before his father returns.

Hannah approaches the old trappers telling them of her plan for a moonlight ride with Ivan, and then asks if they would open the gate. Just to be sure Adolph has left, she asks them if Adolph had replaced his horse that had thrown a shoe and already left for the outpost.

Their answer surprises her, and she becomes more aware of how deceiving Adolph can be. The old trappers tell her Adolph's horse is not lame. They thought he just forgot something. They closed the gate after he left, and Adolph has instructed them not to let her out of the campsite, because he saw a bear cub and its mother close by.

Hannah charms the old trappers into letting her out anyway. They have heard stories from other trappers of how Boris protects her and understand that Hannah knows the ways of the bears and will be able to stay out of trouble.

CHAPTER XI

Escaping the Wrath of Adolph

Hannah leaves campsite and the old trappers warn her again of the hungry bears that roam the tundra. Because the trappers are willing to let her leave, she suspects Adolph does not want to reveal his true intentions to the trappers until he knows he won't have her as his mistress. She decides to stop by the stream to fill her water sack. While at the stream, she looks at the cluster of trees and rocks from where she felt someone had been watching her. She decides to investigate to see if Adolph's returning to the campsite is just a coincidence or if he has planned it, and she waits in the brush till she has gone out to fetch water for her bath.

As Hannah approaches the thicker growth of trees and large rocks at the base of the steep mountain, Shamal becomes skittish. She stops and tries to calm him while looking around carefully for the bear Adolph warned about. She knows how dangerous it would be if she gets between a bear cub and its mother. Hannah looks at the tall grass near the trees and determines it has been trampled on. She can also detect the telltale odor of a bear's den close by. *Is this the bear Adolph warned about?* Remembering Adolf's warning, she thought. She knows not to make any sudden moves to turn around and run back. A bear can easily catch her from the near distance of what could be its den.

Slowly Hannah turns Shamal around and begins to head back for the stream and trail leading back to the campsite. Making her turn, she notices movement out of the corner of her eyes, and a bear cub emerges from the thicket at the base of the trees then quickly stops. Remaining calm, she prepares herself in case its mother also emerges from the thicket and keeps walking at a steady pace, keeping her eye on the thicket. To her surprise, the cub begins to follow and cries out as if calling for its mother. Quickly turning to look in front of her, she can see the cub's mother standing at the stream crossing where she just got water. The bear looks at her, then drops on its four legs immediately charging to protect her cub.

She is not prepared when Shamal rears up and is thrown to the ground. She quickly gets up to see that Shamal is beyond her reach and is running for a clearing trying to avoid the oncoming bear, and she watches as the bear turns quickly to cut off the path of Shamal. She decides to head for the safety of the steep mountains and rocks closer to her than the campsite whiles the bear is occupied going after Shamal.

While running, she hears the snorting and whinnying of Shamal as he kicks and rears up, flailing his hooves for protection. As she climbs a small tree to reach the safety of large rocks on the cliff side not accessible by the bear, she looks back to see that Shamal has gotten away. The bear is now making its way toward her. To be sure she is beyond the reach of the bear, she quickly makes her way through narrow spaces between the rocks, wedging herself in between the large boulders and stepping and holding on to small ledges to climb even higher.

Reaching a narrow ledge enough for her to sit on, she sighs with relief and catches her breath. She can see the mother bear and cub below and remembers seeing the entrance to the bear's den just under the tree she used to climb up on the large rock. Unless she can find another way down, she is trapped where she is until the bear leaves. But it will be very unlikely because of the cub. She will have to find another way down.

The campsite is too far away to call for help. Even if they can hear her, she will not be able to warn them of the bear in time. If they are close enough to see where she is, the bear can see them also. The top of the trees blocks her view of the campsite and the trail leading into the gate. She looks around her for another way down. There is none; except going higher might give her a better viewing point to see more of the mountain's sheer rock face. She had overheard the trappers talk of wild mountain goats that live there and often go down to drink at the stream and graze on grass along the banks. She decides to climb higher and maybe find a way to move along a ledge and hopefully find another way down. The climb up seems easier than trying to move to either side of the ledge she is sitting on.

Carefully, she starts upward, testing every foothold and handhold before committing her full weight on it. It reminds her of how she enjoys climbing on the face of the mountain around the entrance of Herald's cave. Herald had scolded her for climbing above the entrance of the cave and for throwing small pebbles at him when he walked out. He was so afraid that she would fall trying to get back down that he told her not to try until he got Igor and some rope.

She remembers that day as if it is just yesterday. That day, from above the Herald's cave's entrance, she could see and hear Boris as a young cub near the lake, calling out for his mother. That morning, she had seen Adolph and his trappers bring a bear's skin into the stable and hung it up to dry. They talked about the cub that got away, and she knew by his cries, Boris was the cub that had lost its mother. She climbed down easily and ran to Boris, and he stopped crying immediately. Herald and her uncle arrived soon after; amused that she had gotten down by herself. They also knew that Boris was the cub that had lost its mother and were not fearful that they or Hannah were in danger. Herald and her uncle made her promise that if they let her keep Boris, she would not climb up on anything higher than her head again. She recalled it was an easy promise to make for keeping Boris.

Hannah continues her climb with tears streaming down her cheeks as she remembers what Adolph had said about Boris being caught in the steel trap. Looking up toward the heavens, she talks to God as she often heard Herald do. "Please, God," she says. "Herald told me you sent angels to keep children safe from harm, if you had one looking out for my safety, I'm safe now, so can you send the angel to watch over Boris?"

She reaches a ledge high on the face of the mountain, a ledge wide and flat enough for her to rest on for a moment and get comfortable. The ledge is just wide enough so she can rest her feet on it while sitting, and she wraps her arms around her knees after pulling them up close to keep warm. The wind is blowing stronger on the ledge, and she can feel the chill of the coming winter on her face and hands.

She is now high enough to see over the treetops and have an unobstructed view of the trail and campsite. In the camp below, she can identify her tent and the others, and she looks for Shamal to see if he is waiting outside the gate. Hannah hopes he will remain close to the campsite so someone will see him and know she needs help, but Shamal is nowhere close to the campsite.

Her eyes scan the tundra and search the trail leading out of the campsite for Shamal, hoping that the returning trappers will see her horse and know she's in trouble. Hannah is hopeful when she sees a figure resembling a horse far away walking from the campsite toward the next rest stop. "It must be Shamal," she says to herself as she squints to focus. There's no rider on it. Once again talking to herself, sounding hopeful she is right.

From the position of the sun in the sky, Hannah knows it to be just past midday. "Should I try to go down now or wait and try to get someone's attention when they return to the campsite?" She asks herself, wondering what her chances are to be seen or heard. She decides for now she will wait to see if anyone shows up.

Knowing they will reach the campsite easily by day's end, Prince Ezra and his men are discussing their strategy if they encounter any resistance as their horses walk with a high-stepping gait, as if they also are preparing for battle.

Nubar's warning disrupts their discussion. "Prince Ezra! Something is approaching us far ahead." Nubar points forward and stops his horse, and the others also stop to see what it is.

"I see it also. What do you think it is?" the prince asks as he shades his eyes from the glare of the sky.

"I'm not certain, but it looks like a horse. Let's wait for a moment," Nubar suggests, and the others agree. The guards take positions around the prince, and all eyes stare ahead as the figure disappears in a low spot of the trail.

The animal figure slowly appears again; first its head, then its neck, next its chest, and finally its legs. "It's a horse without a rider," Nubar announces, not sounding surprised he is right.

"Let the horse approach. Guards, keep your eyes forward and to our sides in case this is a trick," the prince orders with a calm, soft voice, just above a whisper.

The horse approaches, trotting at first, then walks to a stop, snorting, just ahead of Nubar's horse. Nubar moves closer, reaching for the reins. "Whoa. Easy now," Nubar says softly and slowly grabs the reins. "It looks like the rider was thrown just a short while ago. These reins don't seem too worn by the ground," he says, offering the others an explanation and continues to look the horse over.

Prince Ezra recognizes the horse to be Shamal and calls out to him. Shamal's ears immediately perk up as he looks up toward Ezra and snorts. Ezra speaks in a gentle voice to Shamal to keep him calm.

Then in a slightly alarmed tone, Nubar offers an explanation as to what has happened. "Prince, I fear this horse and its rider were attacked by a bear. It's bleeding on its side where a saddle was once strapped from wounds only a bear could make."

"How serious is the wound?" the prince asks, concerned for the horse. "Just a flesh wound. It should heal if we treat it with what we have for our horses," Nubar replies as he reaches in his bag for ointment they have brought along for that very reason.

The prince offers to help as he dismounts. "Guards, keep watch, I will help." He takes hold of the reins from Nubar and holds Shamal steady as the wound is treated. *I wonder if Ivan survived the attack,* Prince Ezra asks, wondering but not really expecting an answer.

Nubar offers an answer anyway and continues to carefully apply ointment. "Well, Prince, I fear that if the rider was on this horse during the attack and got thrown off because of this blow by the bear, the rider would have died a terrible death. I hope the end came quickly. Perhaps that is why this horse got away."

"Poor soul, I fear you are right once more," says Ezra, feeling sorry and grimacing slightly. "When you're done, let's be on our way and take Shamal to the campsite."

They continue on, now more cautiously because of the recent bear attack. They know the bear could be close by. They also look carefully for any signs of Ivan and occasionally leave the trail to check something if it looks suspicious on the outskirts of the route.

"Prince Ezra! Look there, off to our left," warns the guard on Prince Ezra's left side. "Five men are approaching quickly on horseback."

The others turn quickly and see the men on horseback. Moving together like it is practiced often, the guards move to form a line between their prince and the approaching horsemen. Quickly, they jab their lances in the ground to keep it standing upright within reach and load their crossbows. The horsemen approach within shouting distance, pulling on their reins sharply to stop their horses when they see the guards raise their crossbows taking aim at them.

Prince Ezra shouts out to them. "Please, don't be alarmed. They won't shoot unless you give them reason to. Pardon me for our reception, but I'm Prince Ezra from Arabia, son of King Caspar. We are here to do business for our kingdom and seek out the fur trader named Adolph. Do you know where we can find him?"

One of the men on horseback slightly ahead of the others raises one hand signaling not to shoot and says, "You too need not be alarmed, Ezra. We don't intend to challenge you in battle. You can put your crossbows away. I am Ivan, remember me? These men are trappers who work for my father. We saw you heading for our campsite. Since we didn't expect anyone in this remote area, we were curious to see who you were," says Ivan, hoping to sound cordial and nonthreatening. Ivan could see that the guards look formidable, and they kept their crossbows aimed at them.

Tension rises as no one speaks. Each side restrained, wanting not to provoke the other. Prince Ezra looks directly into Ivan's eyes to see if he is sincere. He sounds truthful enough, but he took Hannah for his mistress just because a dowry was not given. *What kind of a man would do that to Hannah if he intended marriage?* Ezra says to himself, contemplating on what to say or do.

Ezra breaks the silence. "So, Ivan, it is you; then perhaps you can tell us who would be riding Shamal today." Ezra points to Shamal and signals Nubar to move Shamal forward. "We found Shamal just a little while ago heading away from the campsite on the trail."

"Yes, I know who rides Shamal. In fact, my mistress owns him now; I gave Shamal to her for payment. You remember Hannah, don't you, Ezra?" Ivan asks, still pretending as he and Hannah had planned and also wanting to inform Ezra that she is no longer interested in him. However, his voice reveals his concern as to why they have Shamal.

Hannah, Ezra repeats her name in his mind. The prince is shocked by tragic news he has not expected. His breath is frozen, and although his eyes are open, he is blinded by darkness, images in his mind are gone, and sounds of Ivan's voice repeating Hannah's name echo from a distant cave. He closes his eyes and tries to maintain his composure and quickly signals Nubar to take the horse over to them and show them the wounds. His men also feel the anguish, knowing what is going through Ezra's mind. They know Ezra's heart has just been savagely torn open and can do nothing now to help him. The guards are so well trained and disciplined that they don't look back at Ezra. They keep their crossbows aimed forward, waiting for Ezra to regain his composure and command them to put their crossbows away. However, they wish Ezra would give the command to shoot.

It comes not a moment too soon as Nubar makes his way past them with Shamal. "Guards, secure your crossbows," Ezra orders, pretending he is indifferent to what Ivan has said. If not for the distance away from Ivan, it would be easy to see the anguish in his eyes.

Ezra watches for Ivan's reaction as he is shown the wounds on Shamal and while Nubar explains what he thinks happened. From a distance, he can see the fear that is taking over Ivan's face immediately. Without saying anything to anyone, Ivan pulls the reins hard to turn his horse's head back toward the campsite and kicks his horse to a full gallop. The trappers quickly do the same. "We are returning to the campsite to check on what happened!" shouts one of the trappers as he follows the others.

The guards quickly move toward the prince to wait for his instructions and also offer their sincere condolences to the prince in hearing it is Hannah's horse. The prince thanks them but offers some hope. "Let's not rush to judgment in Hannah's demise. I think they rushed off to see if she is in the campsite and if the attack took place there. She may still be unharmed and alive."

Prince Ezra instructs the guide to follow Shamal's hoof prints back to be sure it came straight from the campsite. Nubar agrees it is a wise thing to do. "She may not be at the campsite and could still be alive. Remember that she is very knowledgeable when it came to bears and would have known better to stay out of its way," says Nubar, offering Prince Ezra a reason to be hopeful.

"Once again, I pray you are right," Ezra answers, sounding more hopeful. He instructs one of the guards to remain with Nubar and lead Shamal back, and the other two to follow him to the campsite.

On a cliff near the campsite, Hannah rests, and her body heat generated from the climb has dissipated. The chill of the lofty winds knifes through her clothing, and Hannah knows she can't remain on the ledge through the night. She looks again for another way down. To her right is the way she came up. It will be harder and dangerous going back the same way. Some of the footholds and handholds have crumbled away, and she is lucky not to have fallen. She leans to her left, looking around and down the corner of the ledge. Hannah sees what looked like a narrow trail used by mountain goats to get down to the stream.

Farther over from the ledge she was on, it does not have easy access to the goat trail from what she can see. She leans, lying on her left side, stretching out to see more of the ledge and steep face of the mountain right around the corner. The ledge is narrower, and she's careful not to lose her balance. She looks for handholds and footholds to reach the goat path just below. Far below, away and hidden from the bear's view, Hannah can see the trail end at the base of the mountain. She carefully looks at the footholds and handholds once again to determine if they can hold her weight easily, but can't be certain just by looking. She will have to commit to trying each one carefully as she makes her way. If she falls, she knows she will not survive it, and going down the same way she has come up appears to be the only option. She might fall, but there is a chance she might survive it.

Hannah looks up once more to see if someone is on the trail. Much to her surprise, she can see five men on horses riding hard toward the campsite. She guesses its Ivan and the trappers. They must have seen Shamal, she says to herself. That's why they are running back to the campsite. "Ivan! Ivan! I'm up here!" Hannah shouts as loud as she can and waves her arms side to side in long arcs. She continues knowing they can't hear her over the noise of their horses' hooves. The wind is blowing directly into her face, making it more difficult for them to hear her. She watches Ivan and the trappers ride past and continues to wave her arms, but with much less enthusiasm. Hannah stops waving, realizing that chances of being heard or seen aren't good.

She looks down the right side of the ledge and considers the risk she will take going down the way she has come up. "At least if I lose my footing here, I'll be able to grab on to some of the shrubs growing out of the cracks along the steep mountain face," Hannah says to herself as she takes a few deep breaths to muster up her courage. Glancing up to the trail one last time, she is surprised to see three more horsemen riding hard into the campsite. As she strains her eyes to focus, the wind moves a fog bank into the side of the mountain, blocking her view. "It's just as well. They can't hear or see me anyway. I should try to get down just in case they look for me by the stream" she says to herself, remembering that she can see it from the lower ledge.

Hannah turns her body around and carefully reaches for the first foothold with her right foot. She lowers herself over the edge, with her hands holding her—braced and balanced on the ledge. That wasn't so bad, she says to herself feeling more confident. Slowly, she places all her weight on it while her hands are still above the ledge to catch her if she loses her footing. She reaches for another lower foothold with her left foot, her upper body now beyond the safety of the ledge. She slowly and carefully transfers more weight onto her left foothold with just her fingertips gripping the ledge. Hanging perilously on the edge, she must find another strong handhold just below the ledge. She fears her left foothold will not hold her weight.

The sound of loose rocks falling causes her to freeze. Before she can prepare herself with a better handhold, her right foothold gives way completely. Instantaneously, she loses her handhold grip as her right foot kicks outward twisting her body out of position. She screams, but she doesn't hear herself. Her blood rushes through her body, and she hears her heart beat louder and faster. Her fall seems to be slowing down as her heart beats faster. She can see the treetops and large rocks getting closer. Her body is turning toward the face of the mountain, and she sees a small bush and the lower ledge she sat on earlier. It comes rushing up to her face as she tries to reach for the ledge. She can hear herself crash through the branches of the small bush, and the side of her head hit the ledge under the bush. Before losing consciousness, she sees her lower body fall over the ledge, pulling her off. The blue sky is all she can see, and she loses all sense of feeling, as if she is floating on air. Before closing her eyes surrendering to death, she whispers a short prayer. "God, help me."

Hannah's crumpled body lies motionless after tumbling down the steep cliff stopped only by the large rock she climbed on to escape from the bear. Other large rocks she used to climb higher up the side of the cliff hide her from plain view of anyone. Blood seeps from a wound on her head and trickles slowly on the ground. Moments later, her breathing slows, and she drifts off to a timeless space between life and death, no longer feeling the pain from her injuries and no longer caring about life itself.

CHAPTER XII

The Search

van and his men pull their horses to a sliding stop in front of the gate. Leaving their horses, they quickly open it and rush through on foot to look for the old trappers and Hannah while calling for them. Running into Hannah's tent, Ivan calls for her. Seeing she is not in, he leaves without noticing her note and runs into the old trappers as he steps out of Hannah's tent.

"Ivan! The others told us what happened to Hannah's horse, but she's not here. You didn't see her on the trail?" the old trappers ask, wondering where she can be if she isn't found on the trail.

The old trappers tell Ivan of Hannah's plan to meet him at the rest stop for a moonlight ride. Immediately, Ivan and his men run for their horses at the gate and are met by Ezra and his two guards as they are riding up.

"Did you find her?" Ezra asks Ivan.

"She's not here, I assume you haven't seen her on your way here also, Ezra? The old trappers said I was to meet her at the rest stop about a day's ride from here. Did you see any signs of her, Ezra?"

"No, I didn't, but it was dark and—" he is interrupted by Ivan.

"And she's no concern of yours, Ezra. My father will be back here later this day. You can wait here and do your business with him and leave. You and your men are not invited to stay at the campsite tonight, and tell him I went to look for Hannah." Ivan quickly gets on his horse and leaves.

Ezra tries to stop Ivan to tell him about Herald and Igor on their way from the rest stop but is ignored. "Well, they'll find out soon enough. Let's go in and find out more about where Hannah might be," says Ezra as he signals his guards to follow him through the gate. "Maybe she was hiding terrified or collapsed from her wounds, I don't think Ivan and his men made a thorough search of the campsite," Ezra suggests, sounding hopeful.

Inside the campsite, Ezra speaks with the old trappers, and they tell him of what Hannah had planned and assure Ezra the attack didn't happen in the camp. However, they add that if it did happen close by, which seems highly likely, she could have made it back to the camp without them knowing it. They agree that she could be unconscious someplace close, but out of sight. Ezra asks if they can look around more carefully while waiting for Adolph to return. The old trappers agree but warn them not to enter any tent.

Ezra and the two guards walk to the center of the camp surveying the area. Off to the side away from the others, Ezra notices a smaller tent with articles of clothing he remembers to be Hannah's hanging out to dry. Even though he is sure Ivan has checked her tent, he feels the need to look for himself. He signals his guards that he will go over to investigate while they watch if the old trappers notice.

At the entry of her tent, Ezra quickly checks back for an all-clear signal from his guards before going in. Inside, Ezra recognizes the scent of Hannah. His breath shortens and heart beats faster as he remembers the last moment they spent together in a passionate embrace. Realizing that he may never see her again, he sits on the edge of her bed to pray as he sees Herald do on several occasions. Closing his eyes and bowing his head reverently, he speaks from his heart. "Almighty God of the heavens, I realize you don't know me. But I hope Herald has told you about me. I consider him a true friend. I believed him when he told me about the cave dwellers and the gift for the infant child Jesus who is the Christ and king of us all. I did his bidding without expecting anything in return. I pray to you now to ask if you can help us find Hannah, who is also a friend of Herald, and especially if she is still living, almighty God. And please forgive me for my unpolished prayer. Thank you."

Ezra buries his face in his hands with his elbows braced on his knees, holding back the pain of knowing what may have happened to Hannah. Through his fingers and from the corner of his eyes, he notices a folded piece of parchment paper on the bed. He reaches for it and unfolds it, curious to know if it will be a note from Hannah. Immediately, he determines it is and begins to read it, even though he knows it's for Ivan. As he reads it, he is outraged at what Adolph has done and wonders if Ivan knows of the note. He feels a sense of victory and pride for Hannah, realizing that she did not give in to Adolph even though it meant risking her life to escape. Not wanting to waste precious time waiting for Adolph, Ezra decides to look for Hannah immediately. It is more important to find her if she is alive and keep her from being found by Adolph. He places the note in his shirt and rushes out to join his guards.

Approaching his guards, he finds them looking toward the gate. Outside the gate, a horse-drawn wagon and five riders on horseback approach the gate.

One of the men on horseback calls for the old trappers, and Ezra recognizes the voice as Adolph's. Ezra walks hurriedly by his guards toward the gate along with the old trappers, and his guards quickly pick up their lances and crossbows and follow.

At the gate, Adolph waits impatiently while yelling out orders to the old trappers. "Hurry up and open the gate, you old fools. What do you think I pay you for, and to whom do these horses that block the way belong?"

"We'll be right with you," one of the old trappers says as they hurry to open the gate. "The horses belong to these men who have come to trade for fur," the other trapper explains.

Adolph looks over Ezra and his guards but doesn't recognize them. "Who are you? Don't you know I don't trade here? Now get your horses out of my way and be off. I have other plans tonight," Adolph demands, still not recognizing Ezra.

Ezra steps through the gate in plain view of Adolph with both guards on each side. "Adolph, what plans do you have tonight that are more important than spending time with a prince who would like to trade gold for fur?" he asks, wondering if Adolph will recognize him.

"Gold you say? Prince --- prince who?" Adolph asks.

"Have you forgotten me so soon? I'm Ezra."

"Ezra, well, you're still claiming to be a prince, do you? It doesn't matter to me who you are if you have gold to trade for fur. I'm willing to trade for gold anytime and anyplace."

"Adolph, I have important business to do with you for my father's kingdom, but for now it must wait. We found Shamal on the road without a rider. It looks like a bear attacked him. Ivan and his men ran off to check if Hannah is at the rest stop where she had told the old trappers she would meet him for a moonlight ride. Do you have any idea why she would leave here alone, Adolph?" Ezra asks, trying to remain calm, wondering what Adolph will offer to explain Hannah's leaving.

"Well, you know Hannah. She has a mind of her own. I tried to warn her of a mother bear and cub nearby. Didn't I tell you men not to let her leave?" Adolph asks the old trappers. They agree and admit they shouldn't have let her talk them into letting her out.

"This is a terrible thing to happen to Ivan. Hannah and he planned to marry as soon as we returned to Tobolsk. I hope Hannah will be found alive. We will join in the search before it gets too dark," Adolph offers, hiding his true intentions. He must find Hannah first if she is still alive, or she will tell of his plans to use her as a mistress for himself or his men. Ivan is of no consequence and will do whatever Adolph wants. But Ezra has the capacity to stop him or take Hannah away.

"Adolph, you can look for her where you think the mother bear and cub have their den. I will join my guide to see if he found any tracks leading away from the main trail. If any one finds Hannah, shoot a flaming arrow in the air."

Ezra and his guards mount their horses and ride past Adolph and his men. Ezra stares directly into Adolph's eyes as he rides by turning his head intentionally to see if Adolph's eyes have given away the truth. In turn, Adolph can see that Ezra's demeanor is not intended to promote their friendship. Adolph turns away and directs his men to unload the wagon and report to him at his tent. Now more than ever, Ezra is certain that he must find Hannah before Adolph. He senses that Adolph is not worried for her safety, but maybe more interested in satisfying his immoral desires for Hannah.

Not too far ahead of them, Ezra can see Nubar looking into the marshy grass of the tundra just off the trail. Wondering if he has found Hannah, Ezra spurs his horse to a full gallop and in a short time reaches Nubar.

"Did you find anything?" Ezra calls out.

"I did, Prince Ezra. Shamal's tracks lead back to this point then breaks away from the main trail. From what I can see, it looked like his tracks will head toward the base of that mountain between those trees and stream," Nubar suggests as he points out the direction. "There is one other thing I've noticed, Prince Ezra. Shamal did not carry Hannah and the saddle for very long before the attack. His back was not wet from the saddle and sweat as it should be."

"Good work, my trusted guide. I will go back on the trail so Shamal's tracks will not be disturbed, and you can follow it easily. I will head up toward the stream and the trees from the entry of the camp to see if Shamal's tracks head that way also."

"Very well Prince Ezra. You have learned this skill well. Soon it will be dark, if any sign of her is found, the guards are to signal with a fire arrow. Agreed?"

Ezra agrees and rides back with his two guards.

In the area where Ezra and his men last rested, Ivan and his men find the evidence of a small campfire. "They must have rested here," Ivan suggests.

"Ivan, I know you are anxious to find Hannah," one of his men says. "But we are going about this the wrong way. I don't believe she made it to the rest stop. For a while now and also here, all the tracks lead to the camp. I have not found one leading away," the same trapper says, frustrated with Ivan's hasty decisions.

"Very well, what do you suggest we do now?" Ivan asks, sensing that the men will abandon him.

"Our horses are tired from all the running and so are we. Let's rest here awhile. I will look ahead on foot to be sure Hannah did not pass this point. If not, let's head back before it's too dark. We can gather supplies at the camp to search all night if we have to."

While trying to unsaddle their horses, the horses become very skittish and try to break away. The men are alarmed and quickly look at each other, asking what is frightening the horses. One of the trappers cries out. "A large bear is headed this way on the trail."

"A bear, where?" Ivan asks.

"There, farther up the trail!" The trapper points as he quickly returns to tightening the cinch of his saddle.

"There is only one bear I know of that large in this area, I think its Boris, Hannah's bear, don't panic yet. Get on your horses and be ready," Ivan advises, trying to keep them calm. "There, up farther, I think I see Herald on his reindeer and someone else."

"Hannah's bear, Herald on his reindeer, what are you talking about, Ivan?" one of the trappers asks.

"Be calm and don't run. This bear won't hurt you unless you hurt Hannah or threaten it. Just keep your horse steady and wave a friendly greeting to Herald as I do," Ivan advises as he waves at Herald.

The waving of their hands causes Boris to stop and stand on his hind legs. Boris sniffs the air and looks at them. "You better be right, Ivan, the bear you call Boris doesn't look like it will wave back," says one of the trappers. "If you are so sure, why don't you move up closer so we can see how friendly this bear will be? Isn't he the bear your father set the trap for?" The trapper nearest to the trail asks.

"What do you mean? I have no knowledge of that. How could my father intend the trap to be for Boris?" Ivan replies, a little confused as he slowly moves ahead on the trail.

"I will tell you later. It doesn't appear like Boris is the bear that got caught last night," says the trapper.

Boris drops to standing on all four legs and waits for Herald and Igor to ride up. Ivan recognizes Igor and is surprised to see him away from the stables. He calls out to him first. "Igor! What are you doing here?" Ivan asks, wondering if Igor knows about Hannah's accident.

"Ivan, never mind why I'm here. Where is Hannah?" Igor demands, fearing they have mistreated her.

"Igor, I hoped that you, instead, would tell me where she is. Did you not see her at the rest stop? She left word at the campsite that she would meet me there. She had gone on a ride with Shamal before I got back to camp."

"No, Ivan, we did not see her. Why would she leave the camp alone? She knows how dangerous it is to travel alone in the tundra," Igor asks. "Now where is she? And what have you done to her?" Igor impatiently demands an answer from Ivan.

"Igor, Herald, I'm afraid I must tell you of a terrible accident. We fear that while riding Shamal, Hannah was attacked by a bear. Ezra and his men found Shamal on the trail heading this way with wounds on his side from a bear. We have been looking for Hannah since," Ivan explains.

"Are you sure Hannah was riding Shamal when it happened, Ivan?" Igor asks, hoping it would not be true.

"I fear that is so, Igor. You know yourself that I gave Shamal to Hannah."

"Maybe we would believe you, Ivan, if you tell us why you baited your trap with a piece of Hannah's clothing and trapped Boris," Herald questions as he pulls out the piece of clothing he found and shows it to Ivan.

"I don't have knowledge of that, but I know of someone who does," Ivan says as he turns around to face the trapper who started to tell him earlier.

"Well, speak up. What do you know of this?" Herald asks the trapper who is reluctant to speak. "If you can't find the courage to speak, perhaps you will find the courage if Boris helps you? Boris --- up Boris!" Herald calls out, and Boris quickly rises up on his hind legs and growls. Ivan, his men, and their horses nervously look at Boris who towers over them.

"Stop him! Please stop him! I'll tell you" begs the trapper.

"Boris, down Boris!" orders Herald.

"Adolph made us do it, Ivan. Your father did. He said with Hannah in our camp, Boris would be in the area and would steal from our traps," the trapper replies, still looking at Boris.

"Boris steals from traps?" Igor repeats.

"Adolph knows better. Boris has never taken from trappers since Hannah raised him from a cub. He must have another reason why he doesn't want Boris here, and as her father, I fear it's not a good one. Now tell me all you know, or I will tear your tongue out and feed it to Boris!" demands Igor on the brink of losing his patience and temper.

"Please, Igor, I have no argument with you. Believe me, it's all he said. You know that no one questions Adolph. Why don't you go to the camp and question him yourself?" the trapper suggests, hoping to escape the wrath of Igor.

Igor turns to Ivan. "Ivan, I hope you have no part in this, for I will hold you responsible if anything terrible was done to Hannah that caused her to run off," Igor warns.

"Very well, Igor, I understand your concern. I, too, am curious to know why my father wanted to catch Boris. We should hurry before it is too dark," Ivan agrees and pulls his horse around to head back.

Back at the camp, Ezra sees Adolph having a discussion with his men as he nears the gate. They quickly break up when they see Ezra approach.

Ezra assumes Adolph is organizing his men for the search to look for tracks leading away into the grass beside the trail and follow them on a foot trail leading to the stream. He signals his two guards to join him.

At the stream, Ezra can clearly see Hannah has been there with Shamal and looks around to see where else the tracks lead. While searching, he discovers bear tracks and quickly looks around to be sure the bear is not nearby. Signaling his guards to look to where he is pointing, he continues to scan the area around them across the stream and toward the cluster of trees and mountain. Sensing the attack has taken place nearby, he begins to get anxious. His guards feel the same and load their crossbows. They quickly move ahead of Ezra on both sides as he points out the direction of the bear's tracks leading away from the stream.

Ahead, they notice an object in the tall grass. Ezra identifies it immediately as the saddle and quickly moves ahead looking for Hannah. With night fast approaching, Ezra knows everyone is needed in the area if Hannah is nearby. He orders his guards to send up the signal. One of the guards reaches into a special pouch at his side holding small pieces of cloth soaked in lantern oil and quickly ties one on the tip of his arrow. The other guard lights the arrowhead using a piece of flint and strikes it with a small piece of iron.

As the guard prepares to fire, a loud roar is heard from the cluster of trees. Ezra and both guards turn to see a mother bear and cub in the dark shadows behind the trees.

"Should I shoot, Prince Ezra?" the guard with the lit arrow and crossbow aimed at the mother bear asks.

"Not yet." Ezra waits to see if it will attack. The bear rises up on its hind legs and roars again walking out of the shadows.

"I believe the bear is getting ready to charge us, Prince Ezra," the guard warns.

"Shoot past its head and strike the tree behind the bear," Ezra orders. The arrow knifes through the air with a hissing sound, leaving a trail of smoke. The arrow strikes the tree behind the bear, distracting it and stopping its charge. Ezra and his guards watch closely as the bear drops on all four legs. Its head moves from side to side scanning the area. The bear looks toward the group of men leaving the campsite and notices Adolph and his men moving into the clearing before the stream.

Ezra orders his men to stand fast. The feeling of being more threatened with more men approaching, the mother bear turns around and disappears with her cub around the base of the mountain, occasionally stopping to look back. Ezra repeats his request for a signal and soon after another arrow is lit and flies in a high arc into the evening sky.

Farther up the trail where Ivan and his men, Herald, and Igor are still about an hour from the camp, Ivan stops abruptly. "Did you see that?" Ivan calls out to his men.

"Yes! At the base of the mountain, it must be a signal about Hannah," one of them suggests.

"Igor, we are faster on horses, and we will go ahead," Ivan suggests as he kicks his horse to a gallop.

Back on the trail just outside the gate, Adolph keeps a watchful eye on Ezra since the bear has gotten their attention. Seeing the signal, he directs his men to follow him to where Ezra and his men gather around an object on the ground. Beyond the stream, Nubar also notices the signal and picks up his pace to join Ezra.

Soon, all have gathered around Hannah's fallen saddle. It is now late evening, and darkness in the area is held at bay by flickering torches that are being lit and handed out by Adolph's men. After quickly agreeing on where to search, they form a line to the stream and face the mountain. In a flanking movement, they walk carefully searching in knee-high grass for any clue.

Adolph instead heads directly for the cluster of trees, not wanting to be a part of any organized search led by Ezra. He remembers seeing the cub a few days ago among the trees and decides to start there. He needs to be the first to find Hannah just in case she is alive and make sure she doesn't reveal how he has threatened her.

Not trusting Adolph, Prince Ezra keeps an eye on him while Nubar offers a quick appraisal of what he has found, "Prince Ezra, from what I can see, there was no struggle here. It seems she escaped the attack, or she was not on the horse to begin with when the bear struck," Nubar explains.

"Yes, that's good news, I've come to the same conclusion, let's move forward to where Adolph has disappeared into the trees," the prince orders.

Ahead of them, one of Adolph's men picks up an object from the ground and takes it to show Adolph before Ezra can get to him. He disappears into the trees with Adolph also, and when Ezra gets there ahead of his men, he calls into the thicket.

"Have you found anything, Adolph?" Ezra asks.

"There's nothing in here but a small cave where the bear and her cub rested," Adolph replies. "Come in and see for yourself."

Ezra is anxious to see for himself because he doesn't trust Adolph to tell the truth. He walks into the dark shadows of the trees. A branch is hanging low, and it forces him to stoop over to avoid it. Instinctively, he realizes that he can be walking into a trap, but it's too late, and a blow to the back of his head knocks him unconscious. Ezra slumps to the ground in the cover of the trees and darkness.

"Search him for the gold!" Adolph orders in a forced whisper, trying to suppress his excitement.

"He doesn't have anything hidden on him except for this folded parchment paper," the trapper answers and hands it over to Adolph.

Adolph holds his torch up to read it and while grinning burns the note. He orders the trapper to tie Ezra's hands and feet and keep a knife to his throat, then he steps out of the trees to get the attention of Ezra's men.

"You there, listen carefully and do as I say or your Prince Ezra will take his last breath." Adolph turns around and signals the trapper hiding in the trees to drag Ezra out. In all the commotion, Adolph does not realize one of Ezra's guards is not with the others. He only remembers two that are with the prince and has forgotten about the other guard who arrived later with Nubar.

Ezra staggers as he regains consciousness and kneels on his bound feet. The trapper holds Ezra's head up and stands behind him with a knife at Ezra's throat.

"Your prince speaks of trading with gold. I'll ask you once only. Would you like to trade his life for the gold? Now hand over the gold or else," Adolph demands.

Ezra's men look at each other, not knowing what to say or do.

Adolph's men move in to surround them. Fortunately, they also don't notice the absence of one guard. However, Ezra's guards quickly realize one of them is missing and wait to see if it is noticed. To distract them, Nubar quickly offers an answer.

"Adolph, I can tell you who had it, but I don't know where it was hidden. Only that person can." Nubar waits, stalling for more time, and they quietly talk among themselves, thinking of what to do.

Meanwhile, the missing guard observed everything from the cover of the tree he shot the flaming arrow into. While others formed the search for Hannah, he had gone unnoticed the cluster of trees looking for his arrow out of view of everyone. While working the arrowhead free from the tree trunk, he noticed a few small branches of the tree recently broken off and wondered if it was caused by Hannah climbing for safety. He was distracted when he heard Adolph ride up. Not being sure of Adolph's intent, he remained out of sight behind the large rock forming one side of the bear's den. As he watched, he found it strange that Adolph did not appear to be searching for Hannah, but was waiting instead for someone to join him. A few moments later, one of the trappers did. He heard Prince Ezra call out to Adolph but didn't expect the prince would be coming into the thicket of trees. The guard's view of the prince coming into the thicket was blocked. He heard a thud and a shuffle of branches and leaves, but didn't know what happened until he heard Adolph speak of looking for the gold. At that moment, he could only watch until there was an opportunity to rescue the prince without jeopardizing his safety and the others.

"Well, go on! Speak out!" demands Adolph, growing impatient. "Adolph, I will tell you if you allow us to join you and your men," Nubar suggests, trying to strike a bargain that will perhaps give them an opportunity to save the prince.

"Do you really think you are in a position to bargain for anything?" Adolph scoffs.

"Oh no, Adolph, please forgive me, I don't mean to insult you." Nubar thinks of a ploy to lure Adolph into a false sense of control. "I assumed, Adolph, you would not want me to say out loud so your men will not know also, or do you trust them enough to know they will not go for the gold themselves?" Nubar explains, hoping he convinces Adolph.

Adolph considers his options. "Hmm, you may have a point. Why do you wish to join me and my men?"

"Because we want to be free men like you and trade for our own wealth. Not be slaves and servants all our lives for the likes of him," Nubar answers, pointing to Ezra.

As expected, Ezra shows his displeasure. "You traitor, I thought you would be the most trusted and loyal of all."

"You are a fool to think you can trust us to protect you with all the gold you have taken from our families," Nubar replies in defiance, hoping the guards will hold their silence as he has asked.

Ezra can't believe what he is hearing, until he notices the guards not reacting and reasons that they are up to something. Ezra plays out his displeasure. "You will all pay for this. If I don't return, you know my father will take the life of your wives and children," Ezra suggests, knowing as bachelors, they will understand he is going along with them.

"Ezra, you can no longer threaten us by holding our families hostage. By now they are gone from your father's kingdom. As I said, Ezra, you are easily fooled. And if Adolph lets me, I will slit your throat from ear to ear after you beg for mercy," Nubar threatens, hoping to finally convince Adolph.

Nubar is also relieved that Ezra and the guards are playing along and hopes the other guard, hiding and waiting, will take advantage of the opportunity when it is time.

Adolph is slightly amused at the exchange between Ezra and his most trusted guide. "I know of how gold can't be tarnished, but I can plainly see how it will tarnish the most trusted friendships. I will offer you the opportunity to prove your intentions by letting you take Ezra's head off. To be sure you do, I will have my man stand by your side with one of your crossbows aimed at you."

Adolph calls out to one of his men to retrieve the crossbows from the guards' horses and bring Nubar to him, and then he tells the trapper holding Ezra to make him kneel and bend over.

"Are you ready to die from the hands of your most trusted guide, Prince Ezra?" Adolph asks, taunting him.

"I'm ready, Adolph. But are you? I will show you how a prince can face death as only I can. No one will need to hold my head down. I will bow low and hold my throat into the blade as he pulls it through," Ezra said in defiance. Ezra bows at his waist and waits for Nubar to take up his position.

One of Adolph's men positions himself close to shoot Nubar just in case he changes his mind as Nubar takes the knife from the trapper holding Ezra.

"Do as he wish and let go of his hair. We shall see how a prince can face his death," Adolph orders.

"Adolph, I must ask you one other thing before I take his life. Since I'm not killing him in battle, I must say a short prayer for my soul and my family's so I'm not cursed by his spirit," Nubar asks.

Adolph nods his head, "If you must, to ease your guilt perhaps?"

Nubar begins in his traditional language, hoping Adolph and his men don't understand. To be sure, he speaks of how happy Ezra is to give up his gold to his friend Adolph. He waits for a reaction but sees none and decides it is time to lay out the plan to the guards and Ezra. In a chanting tone of varying pitch and volume, he instructs Ezra to drop flat to his belly at the signal and hold his wrist high so he can cut the rope. He also tells the guard who, he hopes, is hiding to shoot the man closest to him with the crossbow, and he will throw the knife toward the other just after cutting Ezra's hands free. He hopes Adolph and the trappers will be caught by surprise and can't react in time to stop him. Sounding as though he is ending his prayer, he signals the guards and Ezra to get ready and gives the command to shoot as he reaches for the rope around Ezra's wrist. Before Ezra is flat on the ground, Nubar falls on the prince to protect Ezra just as the guard's arrow zips by his head from the dark shadows of the trees. The arrow pierces the trapper with the crossbow between the eyes and exits at the back of his head. He falls limp to the ground immediately.

The other trapper is completely surprised and looks up to see where the arrow came from. During that distraction, Nubar rolls over and throws the knife at the trapper hitting him in the throat. It causes the trapper to drop the crossbow immediately as he reaches up with both hands to pull the knife.

The trapper who is holding Ezra quickly drops his torch that provides light and reaches for one of the crossbows on the ground while Nubar crawls on his knees, looking for the other. The trapper reaches the crossbow nearest him as Nubar recovers the other but finds the arrow has been shot. From the corner of his eye, Nubar sees the trapper raise the crossbow to aim at him but finds it difficult to see through the flickering light of the torch on the ground.

Ezra sees that Nubar is in danger. "Guard, throw your lance!" Ezra shouts, as he struggles to untie his feet.

The trapper is distracted momentarily and quickly looks around for the guard Ezra has shouted to. As the trapper turns to look toward the trees, a lance flies out of the shadows and rips through his chest with so much force, the sound of his ribs cracking and his agonizing scream is heard over all the other fighting going on. Fearing the same consequences from other guards lurking in the shadows, the remaining trappers stop fighting.

Adolph drops his torch to make his escape and runs for his horse. Ezra frees himself from the rope as he watches Adolph grappling for the saddle and reins to mount his horse, but his panicked approach causes the horse to bolt and back away from Adolph's reach.

"Should I go after him, Prince Ezra?" the guard asks, emerging from the dark shadows of the trees on horseback.

Ezra picks up the torches dropped by Adolph and the trapper and hands one to his guard. "Hurry, you must stop him! We need to know what he knows about Hannah's disappearance."

The guard quickly reaches Adolph as he finally mounts his horse. Adolph looks up to see the crossbow is aimed directly at him.

"Do you think your horse can outrun this arrow, Adolph?" the guard asks, looking straight down the shaft of the arrow into Adolph's eyes.

Adolph gulps hard trying to moisten his vocal cord to answer. "Uh, I don't, I don't, think so. Please, I beg you, have mercy," Adolph pleads, knowing this single guard alone, in just a few seconds, caused the death of three of his men.

"Get off your horse and kneel on the ground," the guard orders.

Ezra, Nubar, and the other two guards walk up to Adolph as he drops to his knees. The last of Adolph's men have been captured and tied, and he is now alone, powerless, and not in control.

"What now, Adolph?" Nubar questions, "Am I now in a position to bargain?" sounding as arrogant as Adolph before. He continues, "Bow in the presence of our prince," he orders. "Your life is now in his hands. The punishment for your crime against our prince is to cut your head off, and only after you cry for mercy as we pull your limbs apart with our horses," Nubar says.

"Tell me what you have done to Hannah and where she is, and I will spare your life," Ezra demands, looking down at Adolph, who is cowering in fear and whimpering for mercy.

"I told you the truth, Ezra. I did nothing to her."

"If you did nothing, then what do you make of this letter from Hannah?" Ezra reaches into his shirt but doesn't find the letter. He looks at Adolph suspiciously. "What have you done with the letter, Adolph?"

"What letter do you speak of, Ezra?"

"The letter you found and burned when you searched him for the gold," the guard answers, still on his horse and crossbow pointed at Adolph.

"Then, Adolph, you are worth nothing to me alive. I will not waste time or the horse's energy to pull you apart. Guards, take his head off," Ezra orders, bitter and frustrated at Adolph's persistent lying.

"No! Please! Have mercy, Prince Ezra, your Highness," Adolph cries out.

The sound of a sword sliding out of its scabbard rings out sharp and reverberates in the cold night air, then fades silent. All is quiet as the sword is held high above Adolph's neck, and the torches are shimmering in its mirrored blade. Only Adolph's persistent whimpering is heard above the sound of the crickets. Then, as if in heightened anticipation, there is dead silence as the guard takes his step to bring the sword down swiftly.

"Wait!" the guard on horseback remembers the tree with recent broken branches. "Prince Ezra, please forgive me, but I forgot to tell you what I discovered. The tree that I retrieved my arrow from showed signs that someone climbed it recently to get on the rock. Perhaps it was Hannah escaping the bear. Let's hurry." They all turn and run to follow the guard. In their excitement, they leave Adolph lying motionless on his side and knees folded partially under him. He faints from the sheer terror of his near-death experience.

The guide and Ezra climb up the tree and stand on the large rock above the den. One guard on the ground tosses up torches to them for light as the other two guards remove some of their heavy leather armor to ease their climbing.

Far away on the trail, the torches look like fireflies darting to and fro in the dark. Nearing the camp gate, Ivan and his men notice the torches and head up toward the mountain. Riding through the grassy clearing before the trees, Ivan hears a familiar voice call out to him from the dark shadows.

"Ivan, Ivan, Stop!" Adolph calls out.

"Father, is that you?" Ivan asks, struggling to see who's in the dark.

"Yes, it is I, Ivan. Thank goodness you were not here earlier. Ezra and his men ambushed us and killed three of my trappers.

"What did he do father?" questions Ivan, finding it odd if Ezra has any reason to do that.

"Look there on the ground close to those trees, Ezra ambushed three of my trappers and killed them," Adolph repeats, pointing to the bodies.

"Why would he do that?" Ivan asks, still confused over what has happened.

"Ezra said he came to take Hannah back to Tobolsk. Of course, I told him Hannah is not his responsibility. We left for the camp to get torches, and when we returned, they ambushed us," Adolph explains.

"Ezra will pay for this. What makes him think he can take Hannah away? Men, get off your horses, untie the others, and follow me with your bows and axes. We'll sneak up to them and ambush them also," Ivan orders.

Nearing the camp and also seeing the torches, Herald and Igor veer off the trail. Igor urges his reindeer Recnarp to run faster as Boris lumbers off the trail far ahead of them. Attracted by the flickering torches along the base of the mountain, Boris stops momentarily and stands on his hind legs and curiously looks in the direction of the torches. Herald and Igor find their way easily as the full moon rises high, providing ample light in the open tundra. They head for the torches also following the path Boris took. As they get closer, from a high vantage point across the stream, they see one of Ezra's guards alone with a torch waiting below a large rock and Ezra with his other guards and Nubar crawling above around the large boulders and rocks. Occasionally, they hear them call out to Hannah over the sound of water rushing through the rock bed of the stream.

The lone guard left below with a torch is unaware that Ivan and his men have met Adolph and have freed the other trappers. The cluster of trees conceals their advance, and Ivan directs some of his men to move toward the stream to catch Ezra in their crossfire when they return.

From their vantage point on the opposite bank of the stream, Igor and Herald notice the dark shadows of men moving in the dim light of the guard's torch. While considering where to cross the stream, they notice the movements of the men appear suspicious, and Igor and Herald hide instead of crossing the stream. They are unaware that Boris had found the stream crossing and is making his way back up to where Ivan and his men are hiding, waiting to ambush Ezra.

With his nose testing the scent of the air around and ahead of him, Boris slowly works his way toward the cluster of trees, taking the same route Hannah had taken earlier in the day. With their attention on the guard, Ivan and his men don't notice the large dark shadow approaching them from behind. Holding their bows ready and their posture poised to attack alerts Boris's instinctive sense of danger, causing him to rise and stand on his hind legs and cast his menacing shadow on the ground. His threatening roar startles them and causes Ivan and his men to turn and aim toward the sound, but by watching the guard and his torch, the flame causes their eyes to adjust slowly to the dark shadows behind them. They aim blindly and release their arrows that fly past Boris perilously close, nicking his thick coat. It angers him more as he drops to his forelegs and starts his charge to the nearest trapper. Ivan and the others drop their bows to escape Boris's attack and head for the tree that is used to climb on the large rock. Meanwhile, Ezra's guard who was waiting at the base of the rock realizes the danger and crawls into the small opening of the bear's den, knowing Boris will not fit through it. The trapper nearest Boris is not so lucky to escape. Boris quickly overruns him as he tries to seek shelter between large boulders at the water's edge of the stream. Igor and Herald make a futile attempt to call Boris off but cannot be heard above Boris's roar and the screaming of the trapper.

Above all the chaos, Ezra and his guards hear the roar and screaming and make their way back to the large rock to check with the guard below, but instead they are met by Ivan and his men.

"Ezra, did you find Hannah?" Ivan asks in a demanding tone.

"No, Ivan, we didn't, but what happened? Is it my guard who got attacked by a bear?" Ezra asks, worried that his guard has been killed.

Ivan seizes the opportunity to catch Ezra off guard. "Yes, your guard is injured and is below in front of the cave. We chased the bear away and came up here to tell you. Look over the edge and see for yourself," Ivan suggests, hoping Ezra will fall for his ploy as he turns also to lure Ezra into looking.

Ezra steps forward beside Ivan to look for his guard. Once again, he feels vulnerable like he did when he was ambushed by Adolph, but realizes it is too late to step back. He feels Ivan's hand in the small of his back pushing as Nubar yells out to warn him. Ezra turns from his waist just before losing his balance, drops his torch, and grabs hold of Ivan's shirt firmly.

"If I go, you go with me, Ivan!" Ezra warns as he fights to hold his grip on Ivan's shirt.

"No, I won't, Ezra. Let go or you fall less your arm," Ivan threatens as he fights to keep his balance and reaches for his ax at his side.

Before Ivan can pull his ax from its scabbard, Ezra leans back and pulls Ivan over the edge with him. As they fall over the edge, Ezra lets go, preparing for the impact. He regains control and gets his feet under him just in time to absorb the bone-jarring impact with the hard ground. Unable to stop his forward momentum, Ezra tumbles forward head over heels and comes to a sliding stop on his back on the side of the hill. With the air knocked out of him, he remains motionless while trying to catch his breath.

Above him still on the large rock, he can hear that his men are in close hand combat with Ivan's trappers. Ezra also notices a light from inside of the bear's den and assumes it to be his guard. The only other source of light comes from the bright moonlight and starry skies. It is bright enough to see Ivan lying motionless, either unconscious or dead, a few feet from him. Suddenly, an ominous shadow blocks the light. Without looking up, he hears the deep rumbling growl of a bear as it approaches. In no position to escape, he tries to remain calm and perfectly still. He wonders as the bear gets closer if this is the same bear, they saw earlier coming back to reclaim her den and also the same bear that attacked Hannah. Preparing for the worse, Ezra slowly moves his hand to his side to grip the handle of his sword. Luckily, the fighting above them attracts the bear's attention, and it rises to stand on its hind legs. Ezra decides this is his opportunity to thrust his sword deep into the bear's rib cage and pierce its heart. Suddenly, the bear roars loudly at the men fighting above. Ezra hesitates, recognizing the deep growling sound of Boris.

"Boris, Boris!" Ezra calls out over the growling, hoping it is Boris while still gripping his sword just in case he is wrong. "Down, Boris! Back, back Boris!" orders Ezra. Boris stops and drops to his forelegs. Boris's immense head is directly over Ezra's chest, and he can feel Boris's hot breath as his nose trails over his skin. He realizes his shirt has been torn open in the fall when saliva drops onto his skin. However, Boris seems interested in something on his upper chest, licking it and sniffing it. Ezra at once remembers it is the medal given to him by Hannah. Calmly and softly, Ezra acknowledges Boris's need. "Yes, Boris, the medal is from Hannah. You remember her sweetness as I do," Ezra says, patting him gently on his head. As if he understands, Boris lets out a grunt and licks Ezra on his face.

Igor and Herald have made their way across the stream after seeing the struggle between Ivan and Ezra and calls out to Boris to stop his attack. They realize immediately that Boris is calm and is no longer a threat to Ezra.

"Ezra, are you well?" Herald asks, looking worried.

"Yes, Herald. I think I'm well, but I'm not sure of Ivan. I don't understand why he tried to kill me. Have you seen Adolph? He also tried to kill me."

"Kill you? I knew they were up to something evil," Herald comments, not understanding why but believing Ezra.

"Have you seen any signs of Hannah?" Igor asks, being hopeful.

"No, Igor, but I'm not sure where to look anymore. We checked every possible place at the base of the cliff. There aren't too many places she could hide. My guide is fairly certain she climbed that tree to escape the bear and wasn't injured," Ezra explains, pointing to the tree feeling helpless.

The lone guard comes out of the cave, loads his crossbow, and aims it at one of the trappers still fighting. "Cease! Cease or you feel this arrow go through your heart!" the guard warns. The trappers and guards stop, and soon the trappers are shoved off the rock to the waiting guard below. Nubar and two guards quickly climb down to tie the trappers to the tree and join Ezra. "Prince Ezra, are you injured badly?" Nubar asks, concerned they have failed in their duty to protect the prince.

"No, I believe I'm alright, thanks to the training you gave me when I was just a boy practicing with you and the guards," Ezra comments as he stands up, checking if his legs can take his weight.

"Prince Ezra, I believe you will be interested in what I've discovered on some of the large flat rocks. I can't be sure in this poor light because our torches have burned out, but it would seem something caused fresh dirt and smaller stones to fall on the large flat rocks from the cliffs above," Nubar suggests.

"It was Hannah who would climb the cliff. She can scale the side of a cliff like a mountain goat and found it playful to go as high as she can to scare Herald and I when she was just a little girl," says Igor, sounding hopeful.

Ivan begins to stir and regains consciousness.

"We need more light to find the way up. Let's take Ivan and his men back to the camp and get more torches," Ezra suggests, keeping an eye on Ivan in case he tries to continue the fight.

"You should have killed me when you had a chance, Ezra. If you find Hannah, it will be over my lifeless body before you can take her away," Ivan warns reaching for his axe.

"If that is your wish, then so be it, Ivan," Ezra says as he reaches for his sword.

"Ivan! Ezra! Stop, or you'll cause Boris to kill you instead," Herald cautions, holding Ezra's arm.

"Tell me why you tried to ambush and kill Prince Ezra and his men instead of helping to find Hannah?" Herald asks, upset that the fighting has wasted valuable time.

"My father said he was ambushed by them and that they killed three of his trappers so they could take Hannah away without much resistance," Ivan explains, feeling justified for his actions.

"You do not know the truth, Ivan. You were not here to see what really happened. Your father ambushed me to steal my gold. Your father caused Hannah to leave the camp. Hannah left you a letter on her bed that you did not find. After being knocked unconscious from the ambush, your father searched me and found the letter I intended to give you. It explained what your father did that caused her to leave. I read it hoping it would give us a clue to where she could be hiding. Ivan, I intended to invite Hannah to return with me only if she wanted to. If she still wanted to marry you, Igor has enough gold now to pay your father a dowry and also his debt for the stable."

"That is a likely story, Ezra. What proof do you have for any of it?" demands Ivan, feeling that his father is unjustly accused.

"Then you tell me, Ivan. How is it I know you and Hannah only pretended your courtship? Hannah thanked you for helping her, but your father wasn't fooled. She said your father came back to the camp and threatened to take her for his mistress, or he would turn her over to his trappers this night."

"You speak nonsense. You can't ... ugh!" Ivan is interrupted by Igor's powerful grip on his throat as he struggles to get free.

"This time he has gone too far! Where is your father?" Igor demands, angered and not realizing that he is choking the life out of Ivan who can't breathe.

"Let him go, so he can speak, Igor," Herald suggests calmly.

"H-He returned to the camp," Ivan replies, gasping for air and pointing.

"Ezra, Igor, while you take Ivan and his men back to the camp and deal with Adolph, I'll stay here with Boris to continue the search. Boris's nose doesn't need any light to search for Hannah," Herald suggests, anxious to continue the search.

"I'll also search with you," Igor offers.

"No, Igor, it would be better if you clear up matters regarding your debt with Adolph and Ivan. I will simply stay here and say a prayer to help in our search and let Boris go on his own," Herald insists, hoping to convince Igor not to stay.

"Herald is right, Igor. It would be better so all this fighting will end one way or another," Ezra agrees, no longer trusting them after being attacked twice.

Ezra, Igor, and the guards escort Ivan and his men back to the campsite while Herald heads in the direction of where Boris is searching.

Chapter XIII

The Search Ends

With his height and powerful legs, Boris climbs up the tree and onto the large rock above the den. Herald Watches as Boris appears to be interested in getting beyond and above other large rocks at the base of the cliff. Narrow passages between the rocks, too narrow for a man, but wide enough for Hannah are exposed by the bright moonlight, and Herald wonders if Hannah has gone through them to make her way farther up the cliff. Aware that Hannah will come out of hiding if she hears Boris's roaring, Herald is worried something has happened to her.

Herald decides that now is the time to use his reindeer Recnad once again to help in a special way. Looking for a spot on the rocks above Boris, Herald quickly mounts Recnad and turns his head toward the rock. "Up Recnad … up!" Herald commands.

With a powerful but graceful leap, Recnad and Herald glide up and over the den and Boris, and land softly on one of the large rocks at the base of the cliff. Perched on the rock, Herald looks in the area around him between the wall of the cliff and the rock. From the corner of his eyes, a star like twinkle captures his attention, and there just below Recnad's feet, Hannah's lifeless body lies with her medal exposed to the shimmering light of the stars and the moon.

Herald quickly jumps off Recnad calling out to Hannah. "Hannah, Hannah. Do you hear me, Hannah?"

There is no answer, and Herald's concern is heightened when he quickly checks for her breathing and heartbeat. "No, no, dear God, why did this have to happen? I have done everything you asked. Why Hannah? She is a kind and innocent child. Why Hannah? Dear God, I don't understand." Herald is startled by a strong wind, as if it carried a message. Herald listens to the howling of the wind, whipping through the narrow spaces between the cliff and the rock, and carefully pulls Hannah's limp and lifeless body out onto the moonlight and checks her injuries. From the wound on the side of her head, the color of blood shows clearly on her fair skin. Herald reaches for the water pouch on his side, the same water he used to heal Boris's injuries, water he got from Star Lake. He uses all that is left to cleanse her wound. Bowing his head in reverence and kneeling by her side, Herald begins his prayer, offering Hannah's lifeless body to God. After a few moments of prayer, Herald slowly rises to his feet and mounts Recnad. And now, the moment he dreaded is inevitable. He must inform Igor and Ezra of the tragedy.

Herald and Recnad leap off the rock and soar over the trees, landing gently on the trail outside of the gate. At the campsite, Herald sees Igor and Adolph in a heated argument while Ezra and the guards gather more torches and rope.

"Stop … I said stop arguing! I have found Hannah," Herald says with a sullen look on his face, for once not smiling.

The arguing stops and all eyes are on Herald as he approaches them. "Did you say you found Hannah?" Igor repeats.

"Yes, that is what I said. But it is not good news I bring you. She fell off the cliff and now lay where I found her," Herald answers, finding it difficult to tell Igor everything.

"How badly is she injured?" Igor questions, hoping it is not too serious.

"I'm sorry to tell you Igor, but she did not survive the fall."

Igor is stricken with grief and drops to his knees, grasping his chest as if to keep his heart from breaking. Ezra, too, is overcome by the sad news, but he has prepared himself for this moment. He places a hand on Igor's shoulders to comfort him, and then looks up at Adolph.

"You and your evil ways have caused this tragedy, Adolph. You have committed a high crime against the kingdom of my father. I purchased the stable from Igor, and he and his family is employed by the kingdom of my father as the keeper of the stables and trading post," Ezra explains, feeling he must avenge the death of Hannah.

"You don't have any proof of what I did Ezra, and what gives you the authority to hold me responsible?" challenges Adolph, still not admitting to his wrongdoings.

"I don't need proof, Adolph, and my guards and their crossbows are authority enough. Guards, tie them up, but be sure to empty their pockets of anything they can use to cut themselves free," Ezra orders, fighting the urge to avenge Hannah's death immediately.

The guards do Ezra's bidding as Herald and Ezra offer condolences to Igor. "Igor, Ezra and I share your sorrow deeply, but we must tend to retrieve her body before wolves do. You should stay here and prepare the wagon so we can take her back to Tobolsk tonight if you wish," Herald suggests, knowing Igor is in no condition to scale the cliff.

"Prince Ezra," Nubar calls. "Didn't you say Hannah used a whistle to call Boris? I found this in Adolph's pocket." Nubar hands the whistle to Ezra.

"Let me see that," Igor demands, rising to his feet and grabbing the whistle. "This is Hannah's. Why do you have it, Adolph?" Igor questions as he approaches Adolph. "What did you do to her, you filthy swine? I will kill you now!"

In a rage, Igor lunges toward Adolph and locks his powerful hands around Adolph's throat. Adolph struggles in vain as he struggles to breathe. Ivan and Ezra are powerless in trying to pull Igor's hands away as Adolph slowly loses consciousness and goes limp. Herald steps up to Igor and gently places a hand on his shoulders.

"Igor! Igor, listen to me. Is this how Hannah would want you to avenge her death? Is this the way of peace? Four men and our princess Hannah perished today. There has been enough killing. It is not our burden to avenge the evil doings of Adolph. It is our great and divine Father who will do so in his way and time. Let him be, Igor," Herald suggests, as Igor let go his grip of death, a grip strengthened by years of Adolph's oppressive control and abuse. Adolph gasps desperately for air on the ground after Igor drops him.

"Get the wagon ready Igor, and Ezra, follow me with your best climber and some rope," Herald orders, knowing he has to take charge of the situation before it gets out of control.

At the base of the mountain, Herald pointed to the large rocks high above the top of the trees.

"How did you climb there, Herald?" Ezra asks.

"Oh, it was dangerous and more difficult getting down. I'm not foolish to try it again without a rope," says Herald, not wanting to reveal the truth, hoping Ezra is satisfied with his answer.

Nubar makes his way up the tree, and then continues upward to the large rocks at the base of the cliff by using a rope with a metal grappling hook tied to the end. Nubar signals that he has found her and wraps Hannah's body in a blanket. He ties her to the rope and lowers her gently down to Ezra, who is waiting on the large rock above the den. Ezra gently carries her to the edge to lower her down to Herald. Before doing so, he cradles her in his arms and pulls the blanket from her face, brushing her hair back over her head, displaying her radiant and innocent beauty that has captured his heart. The paleness of her soft skin glows in the moonlit and starlit night.

Why did this happen again? Why am I burdened with this curse? Why did it have to include Andrea and Hannah? Ezra asks himself. He brushes his fingers over Hannah's lips, and then kisses her gently. "Good-bye, my beloved princess, know that I loved you the moment I set eyes on you, and know that I will until my eyes see no more." Ezra takes a deep breath with his face close to the nape of her neck, remembering the sweet scent of blossoms in her hair.

Below, Herald realizes it is Ezra's moment to mourn his loss and bows his head in prayer as he waits. Soon after, Herald hears Ezra call for him to receive Hannah's body. Ezra lowers her slowly to Herald, and Nubar leaves Ezra alone in his moment of grief and joins Herald. They hear the wagon and horses approach as Ezra makes his way down the tree to join them. Before the wagon stops, Igor jumps off and slowly walks toward them, not wanting to believe that it is Hannah wrapped in the blanket in the arms of Ezra.

Ezra offers her lifeless body to Igor. "Igor, my dear friend, I know the sorrow you feel, I wish this time would pass without so much anguish in our hearts. However, it was meant to be. To experience this pain only means we've all shared the love and happiness she has brought in our lives. Yes, we shed our tears. But we have also experienced, the joy, of Hannah, and that is what we shall remember and treasure always," says Ezra, as he lays Hannah gently into the arms of Igor.

"I know you feel my pain also, Ezra and Herald. I thank you for those kind words. I will start out for Tobolsk tonight." Igor turns to take Hannah's body back to the wagon, then he lays her gently on a fur blanket.

"So be it. Igor, we will go with you. You can start out now if you wish. I will gather supplies and my guards, and catch up with you soon," Ezra suggests, remembering that he needs to deal with Adolph, Ivan, and the trappers.

At the campsite, Ezra asks the remaining trappers if they are willing to trade with Igor who will offer a fair price for their fur and also charge them a fair price for supplies. Agreeing to trade with Igor, Ezra sets them free, but he warns them not to test his patience by remaining loyal to Adolph and Ivan. They are instructed to stay and complete the trapping season, and then return to Tobolsk, where Igor will trade supplies and gold for their fur.

Ezra and his men depart the camp with Adolph and Ivan following, hands bound, and their horses being led by the guards. Ezra remembers how much Shamal meant to Hannah and instructs Nubar to bring him along.

They catch up with Igor and the wagon, and all remain quiet as they form a procession on the trail, following the wagon back to Tobolsk. The chill of the night air signals the coming of winter, and they pull their hoods over their heads to shield their face from the cold. Ezra notices the blanket wrapped around Hannah has blown partially off, and the rough trail jerks the wagon from side to side, causing her hand to fall from the crossed position on her chest.

Still feeling as though Hannah needs his protection, Ezra calls out to Igor. "Igor, stop for a moment. The wind has blown Hannah's blanket off. Let me on the wagon, and I'll wrap it better," offers Ezra, as he dismounts and ties the reins of his horse to the back of the wagon. He motions to Igor to go as he steps onto the wagon.

Behaving as though Hannah is just sleeping and trying not to disturb her, Ezra carefully positions himself, kneeling beside her in the wagon to wrap the blanket. A star-like twinkle catches his eye, and he realizes it's her medal, like the one she gave him before he left Tobolsk. Remembering he still has his medal on, Ezra reaches under his coat to look at it. In the palm of his hands, his medal also has a star-like twinkle as Hannah's. It reminds him of how the metal clasp on the box glitters and causes the box to glow and how it has saved him on several occasions. Ezra reaches for her hand to place it on her chest and grips it as though it is a farewell embrace. At that precise moment, both of their medals start glowing like the clasp did on the box. Instinctively, Ezra looks up for the star, but instead of the star over Bethlehem, he recognizes the star of the north possessing the same brilliant light.

A feeling of warmth rushes through his body and into his hand holding Hannah's. His body weakens, and he feels faint and weak. He closes his eyes to brace himself, feeling the agonizing pain of his loss. He feels frozen in time and lost in darkness, like being back in Herald's cave waking from his sleep, but not knowing if he is alive or dead. Not understanding what is happening; he fights to regain consciousness as he did in the cave. His breathing has stopped, and he forces himself to take a breath and call out to her in the heavens above. Finally, it comes forth like a strong howling wind over the tundra, "Hannaaaah!" Ezra yells out, startling everyone. All eyes are on Ezra, and he looks around him, feeling confused and embarrassed, and offers an apology. "I'm sorry I didn't mean to startle you. I was lost in a dream."

Then, in a voice soft and sweet as an angel, "Were you dreaming of me Ezra?" Hannah asks, gently squeezing his hand.

Ezra is startled and jumps back. "I must still be dreaming!" Ezra tells himself out loud, believing that he has heard Hannah and looks around to see if anyone else has heard her.

"If it is a dream, then I must be in heaven if you are here with me, Ezra," Hannah says once more in her soft and delicate voice, but this time, raising her hands slowly, inviting Ezra to help her up. It is undeniable. Ezra is speechless, his eyes seeing but not believing. On his knees beside her, he is unable to respond, unable to comprehend the miracle before him, but clearly able to comprehend the radiant beauty of her smile.

The others assume what they hear is Ezra talking softly to Hannah and leave him alone to grieve personally. Igor, however, senses it is more than just Ezra's outpouring of grief, as he rubs his bristling hair on the back of his neck, which is causing a strange sensation. Stopping the wagon, he turns around to see what is going on. "What is wrong, Ezra? You look like you've seen a—" Igor stops, noticing Hannah's hand is held up. He watches Ezra cautiously reaching out for Hannah, not sure what he is seeing is true. Ezra's hand touches hers, and slowly, Hannah's fingers grip Ezra's hand.

"Hannah, you're alive?" Ezra asks startled, still not sure if he is not dreaming.

"I won't be sure unless you kiss me, my prince," Hannah replies demurely, as she pulls him gently toward her.

"Hannah … you're alive!" Igor said, startled with his eyes wide open in disbelief, but not expecting an answer as he realizes he is not heard or noticed by Ezra or Hannah.

Ezra slowly and gently pulls Hannah to her knees as their arms embrace. Then believing the moment is real, they kiss affectionately under the bright starlit night of the tundra.

Igor is exuberant and announces to everyone that Hannah is alive, and they all gather close to the wagon, admiring and cheering for Prince Ezra and Hannah, except for Adolph who watches and sneers from a distance under the watchful eye of a guard. Ivan smiles and whispers to himself so his father will not hear him, "I'm happy for you, Hannah, you deserve to be happy with someone you truly love. Go in peace and good fortune, my sister."

Herald is the first to offer a proclamation to capture the moment, "Here ye all! We have witnessed a miracle of life. Let this moment always remind you of the power of prayer and faith, the power of good over evil, the power of love and selflessness, and how our Father in heaven will reward those who have faith and who honor those beliefs."

With Hannah appearing to be completely and miraculously healed from her fall, they decide to press on to Tobolsk, stopping only occasionally for a short rest and tea. Hannah tells of her ordeal with Adolph, and Igor promises that Adolph will pay for the rest of his life.

Daylight brings an unexpected surprise to all, especially Hannah. From a safe distance, Boris approaches them, accompanied by the mother bear and cub. Hannah understands that the mother bear is Boris's mate and cub his, but she knows she cannot approach them. She senses she will never see Boris again. With tears blurring her vision, she watches Boris and his family run back into the open tundra.

They reach the outskirts of Tobolsk, and Prince Ezra stops by the cave, directing his men to pick up samples of rock that came from the star. At the stable, Ira and Igor hold a small celebration for Hannah's return and engagement to Prince Ezra, and preparations to leave on their return trip will start immediately after the celebration. Prince Ezra's servant Nicholas is offered charge of the king's share of the trading post if he chooses to stay, and he happily accepts the responsibility with Igor and Ira. Nicholas is given the authority to use the king's profits anyway he sees fit to spread goodwill and help those in need, hire those that need work, and especially to help the children of Tobolsk. Adolph and Ivan are stripped of their collection of valuables and property and returned to the families he forced to become beggars and servants.

Before the harsh winter season settles into the valley, Prince Ezra, Hannah, and his men depart for Arabia. They leave knowing that Tobolsk will prosper in calm and untroubled tranquility, with happy families, and free from tyrants like Adolph. From that time on, the star of the north becomes brighter and serves to remind everyone how peace and the spirit of giving selflessly will overcome evil, bitterness, and despair.

The return of Prince Ezra and Hannah is highly anticipated and celebrated by all. His family and the people of their kingdom fall in love with Hannah immediately and there is little doubt Prince Ezra and Hannah are meant for each other. On the first anniversary of the trip to Bethlehem, Balthazar and Melchior arrive to join in their Christmas celebration as proclaimed by Caspar to commemorate the birth of Jesus and the marriage of Prince Ezra and Hannah.

THE END

(Back Cover Teaser)

This is a road-twisting, cliff-hanging, gut wrenching, heart-breaking, quest-driven story that whip-cracks the struggle between good and evil.

Was the star over Bethlehem more than just a star that appeared on a celestial clock, or was it on a divine clock that ushered in peace for the warring cave dwellers, and guided a prince to discover fragments of that star, and becomes a tool for the oracle in a cave to prepare the way for the birth of the Christ child?

Will the prince complete his quest for peace after surviving the bitter Siberian Mountains and marching through the deep burning sun-parched sands of the slave-trade wastelands? Can he defeat the ruthless fur-traders, evil-stinking robbers, and mean-as-hell soldiers after being smitten by a ravishing beauty of a Siberian princess? Or will her ferocious Siberian grizzly guardian ravish him instead? …and what of the mysterious oracle who lives in the foothills of the Star Lake region wandering the dark halls of his candlelit cave telling stories of ancient warring cave dwellers and a fiery star? What role does he play in this tale of wonder and treachery, "The Promise of Christmas"?

Discover how St. Nicholas and his flying sleigh and reindeer had its origins with the prince and his family…and how was first celebrated to include the building of the sleigh and why it flies in the Sequel, "The Sleighmaker"